Rise to Power

**Lock Down Publications and Ca$h
Presents**
Rise to Power
A Novel by *T.J. Edwards*

Rise to Power

Lock Down Publications
P.O. Box 870494
Mesquite, Tx 75187

Visit our website @
www.lockdownpublications.com

Copyright 2019 Rise to Power

First Edition March 2019
Printed in the United States of America

Lock Down Publications
Like our page on Facebook: Lock Down Publications @
www.facebook.com/lockdownpublications.ldp
Cover design and layout by: **Dynasty Cover Me**
Book interior design by: **Shawn Walker**
Edited by: **Kiera Northington**

Stay Connected with Us!

Text **LOCKDOWN** to 22828 to stay up-to-date with new releases, sneak peaks, contests and more…

Thank you.

Submission Guideline.

Submit the first three chapters of your completed manuscript to ldpsubmissions@gmail.com, subject line: Your book's title. The manuscript must be in a .doc file and sent as an attachment. Document should be in Times New Roman, double spaced and in size 12 font. Also, provide your synopsis and full contact information. If sending multiple submissions, they must each be in a separate email.

Have a story but no way to send it electronically? You can still submit to LDP/Ca$h Presents. Send in the first three chapters, written or typed, of your completed manuscript to:

LDP: Submissions Dept
Po Box 870494
Mesquite, Tx 75187

DO NOT send original manuscript. Must be a duplicate.

Provide your synopsis and a cover letter containing your full contact information.

Thanks for considering LDP and Ca$h Presents.

T.J. Edwards

Chapter 1
Kaleb

I closed my fist and blew my hot breath into it. It was so cold, my toes felt like they had broken off inside my Timbs. Every time I breathed, it was like I was swallowing a bunch of needles. It was one of the harshest New York winters ever recorded. The snow crunched under my boots as I backed up and took my shirt off. Wiped the blood from my lips with the back of my hand, and spit a nice portion of it into the white snow. I took my shirt off and held my guards in front of my face, already out of breath, but refusing to surrender. Sheek puffed on a fat cigar filled with weed and cocaine. His long dreadlocks fell down his back and over the leather Gucci jacket he wore. He stepped in between myself and Buddy, and looked from me, over to the panting Buddy. Smoke seeped out of his mouth from the cold as he started past Sheek to mug me.

Sheek snickered, taking a long pull from his cigar and inhaling it deeply, before blowing the smoke toward the sky. The wind took ahold of it and whisked it into the heavens. "Yo, one of you lil niggas dipped into the funds. I'm twenty-two hunnit dollars short. Either one of you clowns gon' admit to what you did and accept your consequences like a man, or y'all gon' fight all night until one of you don't get back up. That's my word. We don't steal from one another in this mob. We're a family. We eat out of the same bowl. That's what Blood mean. You feel me?" He mugged me, and then Buddy. Buddy was about five feet nine inches tall, and heavyset. He was dark-skinned, with short dreadlocks. Me, I'm six feet even. Weigh a hundred and eighty-five pounds. Caramel-skinned, with gray eyes my mother passed down to me from her side of our Haitian family. My dreads were in the middle of my back, and had been ever since I was about five years old.

My mother had kept them trimmed so they stayed just in the center of my back, and I'd maintained that style. I took another step back and closed my fists even tighter. They felt frozen. We were in the back of Sheek's brownstone out in Harlem. Sheek was the head Blood in charge of our hood, and had basically been the only father I've ever known. I looked up to him, and aspired to be hood rich, just like him. Buddy spit a bunch of blood into the snow, and coughed, took his asthma pump out of his right front pocket and took two whiffs of it, before replacing it. "Yo, Sheek. Son, you know I don't get down like that. I ain't got that snake shit in my blood, Dunn. Twenty-two hunnit ain't worth stealing. I got loyalty. Word up." He spit another round of blood into the snow. The yard was packed with twenty other members from our crew. All were suited up to brave the elements of the cold. They had us in a circle, which was standard for brawls like the one I found myself dead smack in the middle of.

I knew without a shadow of a doubt, each one was carrying a firearm and on command from Sheek, would shoot us down in the snow with no hesitation or remorse. I'd grown up around most of them, and all of them were cold at heart. "Yo, Sheek, if this what it gotta be, then let us finish this shit, money. My word, I ain't never stole from you a day in my life. And, if he's saying the same thing, then let us battle to the death. I stand firm as a man on my square. If I die, bury me a G." I kicked my shirt aside and guarded my chin, making my way toward Buddy. Sheek stood back and smiled.

"Let's get it on then, niggas. Ain't nobody leaving until somebody is dead. Let's get it."

Buddy frowned and balled his fists. We had been cool ever since the fifth grade, when both of our families moved out here to Harlem, from other boroughs. Mine had come from Brooklyn, while his came over from Queens. It was rough the first year at school, because all of the Harlem kids were real mean. They didn't take to outsiders too well. Because of this, me and Buddy wound up fighting or being jumped every day at recess, or after school, until we finally started fighting together. We eventually became real cool. He had never been my enemy, until this night. This night, it was either him or me, and I wasn't ready to die. "Yo, tell Sheek it was you, son. Tell him right now or I'ma buss ya ass," Buddy threatened, moving closer toward me. I was done talking. I was ready to whoop this nigga, and get away with my life. My mother lay in the hospital, battling cervical cancer.

I had a little brother and sister I needed to care for while she was struggling to get healthy. My father was a deadbeat. Outside of my mother, my family was either addicts, low-lives, in prison, or just didn't give a fuck about my mother and siblings, so I had to make a way every day. It was the only way we were barely surviving in a world so cold. "Enough talking, niggas. I wanna see some more blood. I need to be witnessing a murder right the fuck now. Word up," Sheek hollered, punching his fist into the palm of his leather gloves.

Buddy rushed me and swung, connecting with my jaw. This first blow rocked me to my very core. I saw a blue light and got dizzy. Stumbled backward, trying to regain my senses, but everything was spinning. Snow flew into my face, before melting against my hot skin. My throat felt tight.

9

"Bitch-ass nigga, let's get it in! I ride for my rag, nigga." I shook my head as hard as I could and felt like throwing up.

Then, Buddy was grabbing me into a bear hug, and flipping me on my back in the snow. A bunch of it popped up and landed on top of me. I was expecting for him to straddle, and pound me out. But instead, he stood up and got to jacking as if the fight was over. "I told you, Sheek. Son can't fuck wit my bidness. I told you, Blood. Yo, I don't know if he stole that money or not, but my job here is done. That nigga is out like a light." The world continued to spin. My jaw felt like it was broken. Every time I tried to open my mouth in the slightest, the pain was so unbearable that it brought me close to tears. It was three o'clock in the morning and there I was, laying on my back in the middle of the back yard, fucked over. Sheek took a nine millimeter pistol out of his waistband and pressed the barrel to Buddy's forehead.

"Blood, you ain't done until I say you're done. Kid still got life inside of his body. Take it out. The penalty for stealing from this mob is death. Blood in and Blood out, lil nigga. Now, finish him! Go!" he ordered, cocking the hammer on the gun. I made my way to my feet and held my jaw. Snow dripped off of my naked flesh from the waist up. I was freezing, but I was so mad I couldn't even feel it. I spit a loogey into the snow, and held up my guards.

"Nigga, it ain't over."

Buddy ripped his shirt off of his body as if he were Hulk Hogan or somebody. Threw it to the ground and pointed at me. "I'ma finish you once and for all, nigga. Take this shit back to Queens. Arrgh!" He rushed me at full speed, with his head lowered. My heart started beating fast. I waited right until he was five paces from me, before I jumped in the air with my knee poking out. The bone caught him in the center of his face, bussing his nose and crunching the bone. He covered it with his hands and hollered out on pain. Blood oozed through his fingers and dripped to the all-white snow.

He removed his hands and looked at them, and seemed to freak out. "You broke my nose, Kaleb! You broke my fucking nose!"

"Rush that nigga, Kaleb. Somebody gon' die tonight. It's either you or him," Sheek reminded me. I rushed Buddy, and caught him two hard times in the ribs, took a step back, and kicked him right in the chest, knocking him backward. He fell and rolled to his side, struggled to get up. More blood oozed out of his nose. It dripped off his chin. He got to his feet and threw up his guards again.

"Come on, nigga. Kill me. I'm ready to go." He rushed me, swinging wildly. His first blow connected with my left eye, the second one my jaw and the third one, my chin. Then, his arms were wrapped around my body. He head-butted me in the face and dropped me to the snow. Kicked me in the ribs and flipped me on to my back. "This ain't right, Sheek! Don't make us do this shit. This my mans," Buddy hollered over his shoulder. I threw up a bit in the snow, and jumped to my feet as fast as I could. The snow was coming from the sky like confetti. I could barely see across the yard to Buddy. The wind's speed increased. My dreads blew. My face felt numb. I moved in on Buddy once again, this time much more aware of his capabilities. As soon as I was in the attack zone, I got to swinging to knock him out. I needed for this to be over. I didn't like fighting my mans, but I couldn't die tonight. I was sure Sheek was going to murder the loser. I'd witnessed him do it three times before, and each time my mind had been blown. I punched Buddy hard in the side of the neck.

Then, a jab caught his chin. This sent him staggering backward. I lowered my head and rushed him as fast as I could, picked him up in the air, and slammed him to the ground, and straddled his body. Hitting him with a left, then a right, then a left, then a right again. Back and forth, repeatedly. His head ricocheted off the ground, and I kept on punching, now in a faraway zone. His blood popped up at me, yet it didn't detour me from spurring on, hitting him with everything I had. His eyes were wide open, unblinking as blow after blow pummeled his face. After what seemed like a hundred straight punches, I felt myself being pulled off of him by two of the older Bloods. They threw me to the snow, and stood over me. My chest heaved up and down. My adrenalin was pumping so furiously through my veins, I lashed up at them. Sheek stepped over me and smiled a crooked grin. "It's over, nigga. You fucked him up. That's all I wanted to see, but calm yo lil ass down," he ordered, reaching with a hand out to help me up.

I accepted it and stood up, breathing hard. As my adrenalin faded, the fact that I was shirtless became apparent. Now, I was freezing cold. My teeth chattered. My knees knocked together and my jaw felt like it had been crashed into by a bus. I looked over at Buddy and saw him struggling to sit up. His face was a bloody pulp. He groaned and made noises that told me he was in agony. All of a sudden, my sympathy for him kicked in. I wished it had never come to this. My ribs started to ache. I put my arms around them and looked up at Sheek. "Yo, what now, money?" I asked, gritting my teeth. I need to pop a Percocet or some type of pain killer. I was screwed up and hurting. Sheek sucked his teeth, looked over at Buddy, then handed me his pistol.

"Finish him, kid. You know how the game go." I continued to hold my ribs, looking up at him.

"Yo, I fucked him up enough, son. Just let us hussle and get the money that you're missing back. Don't make me murder my mans over twenty-two hunnit, Boss!" I winced in agony. All of the Bloods closed in on me and took out their pistols. Sheek looked around and smiled.

"Blood in and Blood out, lil nigga. I'ma say this one more time, it's either you or it's him. Which is it going to be?" He curled his lip and slapped the gun to my chest so hard that I took two steps backward. I took the gun, holding it in my hand, looking down at it. I turned around to face Buddy. He was on one knee, with blood dripping from his wounds. He struggled to get to two feet, then fell back down to one knee.

"Yo, this shit ain't cool, Sheek. Don't do this, man. I been running under you ever since I was eleven years old, money. You're like my pops."

"Kill that nigga, Kaleb. Do it now. This my last time telling you. Slime, if he don't pull that trigger in the next ten seconds, everybody's guns turn on him and shoot on my command."

They nodded their heads, and I could see the looks of readiness all over their faces. This worried and vexed me at the same time. I lowered my head then raised it, pointed the gun at Buddy. "Yo, I'm sorry, kid. I got mad love for you, Dunn. I got your son forever, my nigga. That's my word."

Buddy shook his head. "Don't do this shit, Kaleb. This ain't right, man. You know I'd never steal from Piru. We live and breathe this Blood, nigga. Look at me. Look at me, Kaleb. I'm fucked up, man. You fucked me up, now you gon' kill me? Really?"

"Ten, nine, eight, seven, six, five, four, three, two, one," Sheek began his countdown. As soon as he got to one, all guns were turned on me. "Now I'ma count down from ten one more time, and when the clock runs out, the bullets spit out! If we gotta have two dead niggas, then so be it. Ten, nine, eight, seven..."

Buddy turned to face me. His arms wrapped around his ribs. "Do it, son. Fuck it. Ain't no sense in both of us dying back here. Just keep my son straight. Don't let just no any nigga raise my seed, Kaleb. I'll see you on the other side, Dunn. Shoot."

"Damn, nigga." I stepped forward and pressed the barrel to his forehead and pulled the trigger two quick times, expecting the gun to jump in my hands. When nothing happened, I looked down at it and tried again. But, nothing happened. Sheek pulled me backward and yanked the gun out of my hand. "I just wanted to see if you had the heart, nigga. You good wit me." He wrapped his arm around my neck. "Yo, take Buddy ass in the basement and cut his right hand off, then drop him off at the hospital. That's an order." The gang rushed over to him and snatched him up. Forcibly, they drug him across the yard, while he begged them not carry out Sheek's order.

"Yo, I never for one second thought it was you, kid. I don't see that snake shit in you like I do Blood. I shoulda let you kill ya mans, but that would have fucked you up for life. Trust me on that one." He picked my shirt up from the snow and tossed it to me. "The penalty for theft is murder, but on the strength of you, I'ma let ya mans live and give him this one-time pass, but you owe me. Nah' mean?" I slid my shirt over my body and nodded.

"Yeah, I know what you mean." I handed him back the gun, and watched him place it on his waist. He walked to the back alley, until we were alongside of his brand-new Benz truck. He opened the door and reached under the seat, pulled out a purple Crown Royal bag.

"Huh, this nine ounces of that Boy. I need you to drop this off to my mans in Manhattan before five. Tomorrow, you meet wit me and I got some other shit I need you to handle. Feel me?"

I took the dope and nodded. "I feel you, god. Yo, but do they really need to cut Blood's hand off? I just don't think kid dipped in the cookie jar like that, Dunn. It ain't in neither one of our character." I hated to imagine Buddy without his right hand. I knew that was going to turn his world upside down. If I could have prevented it, I would have.

"Yo, don't worry about him. He gotta take his consequences as a man. That's how the game goes. You just do like I said. I'll text you the address in twenty minutes."

Chapter 2

I held my mother's forehead as I ran the clippers over her scalp. She sat still, humming an Isley Brothers' song to herself. They had the heat turned all the way up in her hospital room. She had a problem with being cold ever since she'd started her chemotherapy. After I finished with the last portion of her head, I turned the clippers off and rolled the cord around the body of them. "There you go, Moms, you're all good to go." I kissed her forehead, and felt a sense of sickness course through me. I hated that my mother was battling cancer. I hated to see her sick all the time, hated to think about losing her every second of every day. She slid out of the chair and took a small mirror out of her purse. Looking herself over from every angle, speaking French to herself, then laughing.

"Well, baby, at least I make this style look good." She replaced the mirror, and sat on the edge of her bed. I put the clippers into my book bag, and sat beside her. Wrapped my arm around her shoulder, and kissed her cheek.

"You make everything look good, Momma. I can't wait until they release you from here. I wanna take you out to dinner and spoil you a little bit. You deserve to be spoiled. You know that?" She smiled, and nodded.

"Oh, son, you're preaching to the choir. You know I know I deserve to be spoiled. I am a queen. Don't let this bald head fool you." She joked and coughed into her fist. "Were you able to come up with some of the money I need for my treatments?" She said this and laid her cheek against mine.

"How much did you say that we needed to give them a week?" I asked, knowing good and well the amount.

"Four thousand, baby. I've already given them the eighteen hundred that you gave me yesterday. We're down twenty two hundred. That's what I need before they go on to the next step." She broke into a fit of coughs, and laid her face on my chest.

I patted her back and dug into my jean pocket and pulled out twenty-two, one-hundred-dollar bills. "I got it right here, Mama." I handed it to her and kissed her soft cheek again. I loved my mother with everything I was. She had been both my mother and father for as long as I could remember, and she'd done one hell of a job at being both. She slid from my embrace and looked up at me.

"Son, is this all of it?" She peeled the money open and began to count it bill for bill. Her gray eyes getting more and more bucked, the more she counted.

"Yeah, that's twenty-two hundred on the head. I had to pull a dirty stunt in order to get it. It sucks, but you come first. I'll right my wrongs later. Nah' mean?" She looked into my eyes and exhaled.

"Do I wanna know?" I shook my head.

"Nall, but you know I'ma tell you anyway. I don't keep nothing from my queen." I kissed her forehead. "Sheek sent me and Buddy on a run out to New Jersey. We were to drop off a kilo of heroin and pick up forty thousand. During the transaction, I cuffed twenty-two hundred. Long story short, I refused to cop to the indiscretion. Me and Buddy wound up fighting in Sheek's back yard. I won, and they cut Buddy's right hand off."

She covered her mouth. "Oh, my God. Lord, have mercy."

"Yeah, I know, but it is what it is. I'll find a way to make it up to him." I knew that statement was nearly impossible. All I could do was the best I could. I'd been feeling like shit for three days, ever since I found out Buddy's hand had actually been cut off. I still had not been able to face him and didn't know when I would be able to.

My mother looked down at the money and shook her head. "I feel so horrible taking this money, knowing where it has come from. Baby, I don't want you risking your life like this for me. I will be okay. I've been fighting this long. What makes you think I'll give up now?" she asked, getting out of the bed and pacing the floor. I jumped up and frowned.

"I'ma fight for you until I ain't got no more breath in my body. You're my queen. I'll die for you. Ain't nobody gon' go harder for you then I will. You understand that?" I pulled her into my embrace and wrapped my arms around her small frame. Holding her and not wanting to let her go. Every other thought was of her present physical state. I just wanted her to be healed already, wanted my mother back. The thought of losing her was too much for me to bear.

I knew I would lose my mind if I ever did. She shook her head. "I don't understand where you get all this valor from. Your father is the worst human being I've ever known. I fell in love with the animal in him, and not the man. I regret everything about him. Everything, except for the blessing of you. You're the greatest gift any mother could ever ask for. I don't know what I would do if I didn't have you in my corner, son. I mean that." She hugged me and then kissed my lips, before laying her head on my chest.

"You never have to worry about not having me. I'ma hold you down like a man is supposed to. You're my heart, and I got this." I felt my eyes watering, and this only angered me. I didn't like shedding tears ever my mother. I felt like tears were for mourning the dead, not the living. And my mother was alive and in my eyes, always would be.

There was two knocks at the door, and then Rayven stuck her head inside the room. "Hey, Mama, I know I'm dropping in without asking, but I needed to see you." She stepped fully into the room, with a bouquet of red roses. The scent of her perfume entered as soon as she did. It smelled lovely. Rayven was five feet six inches tall, Asian, black, and Puerto Rican. She had long curly hair that flowed down her back. Juicy lips, and a body that looked like she'd paid for it, but I could vouch it was all real. She'd been strapped her whole life. I met her in the sixth grade at Jackie Robinson Middle School, and she'd been stacked even back then. Now at the age of eighteen, her body had only gotten better with time. Rayven and I were what you called on and off again companions.

She was my woman, but at the same time, I wasn't trying to lock her down and she knew she couldn't lock me down either. We each had our own individual goals we were trying to accomplish, goals that would help us to break out of the slums of Harlem. Even though I wasn't trying to stop her from doing her on any level, I still cared a great deal about her, even though I rarely expressed that truth to her. I wasn't the type to wear my heart on my sleeve. I felt like people took advantage of those that expressed their feelings, so I kept mine inside, unless I was with my mother. She was my only safe haven. My mother broke our embrace and waved Rayven over.

"Come here, baby. It's okay. You ain't always gotta have an invitation to come and see me. You just warmed my heart." She said the last part in French. Held her arms open for Rayven to walk inside them. Rayven was rocking a tight Prada jean 'fit that hung to her every curve. When she wrapped her arms around my mother, she couldn't help but to stick that big booty out. It sat righteous at the top of her thick thighs. Her Alexander McQueen boots were attached to a three-inch heel. This caused that backside to toot up a little further. I felt a stirring down below and had to look off. I knew I would be climbing between them thighs real soon. There was no way around that. They finished their hug, and then she kissed my mother on both cheeks.

"How are you, Mama?" she asked, reaching inside her bra and coming up with a roll of fifties. She handed it to my mother and popped back on her legs.

My mother's eyes got big. She took the money and began to count it. "I'm feeling better, baby. A little nauseous, but better nonetheless. What is this for?" She looked up at Rayven. Rayven shrugged her shoulders.

"Just because. I had a good night at the club yesterday, and I wanted to make sure I blessed you with something. I know they're robbing you. Charging you four thousand dollars a week for your treatments. That's unfair. I have to do my part. You're my mother. And you've been the best mother I've had, ever since mine left me in the projects to fend for myself at twelve." She lowered her head and shook it. My mother finished counting the money, and held her arms open.

"Come here, baby." She hugged her, and patted her back.

"Yo, what about the god? Ma, you acting like you don't see the kid right here. What's good?" I was feeling some type of way. You see, every now and then Rayven acted a little funny toward me, or at least that's how I felt. She worked at a real uppity strip club out in Manhattan.

Being out there, she rubbed shoulders with some of the richest people on earth. Being that she was so fine, they never hesitated to flood her with compliments, or offer her the world for one night of action. I felt like this sometimes put her head up in the clouds. She was a round-the-way girl that more often than not, thought she was too good for the average project dude. Due to the fact that I didn't have my chips all the way up as of yet, I sometimes felt inadequate in her presence. I didn't know what was going through her head, and this kept me on edge. In New York, you were only given respect by your net worth, and currently I didn't have one. This made me feel like a chump, less than a man.

She looked over her shoulder and smiled. She looked even finer when she smiled. "Dang, Kaleb, give me a chance to show my love to Mama. I'ma get to you in a minute." She rolled her eyes and snickered. I ain't like that.

"Nall, ma, you speak to me as soon as you recognize the god. Nah' mean?" I walked over and grabbed her arm, pulled her into my embrace. "Ma, you might wanna turn your head real quick." My mother waved me off and turned her back anyway.

"Whatever, boy." She recounted the money and acted as if we were no longer in the room. I rubbed my hands all over Rayven's round ass and cuffed it. Kissed her lips, and sucked them into my mouth. Her lip gloss tasted sweet. Being this close allowed me to enjoy the scent of her perfume. She felt so soft and warm in my arms. Her long hair flowed over my arms that were clasped around her lower back. She moaned into my mouth, and slid her tongue between my lips. Turned her head to the side and kissed me harder. "Dang, Kaleb, you know we shouldn't be doing this while your mother is in the room. Mmm." She tilted her head back.

I kissed all over her neck and bit into it. Sucked hard and ran my tongue up to her earlobe. My grip on her ass intensified. I wanted some of her body. I was feening for it. "Damn, shorty. You got me feeling some type of way like a muh..." I caught myself, knowing my mother was in the room. Reluctantly, I broke our embrace and adjusted my hard manhood that was poking up in my jeans. I flipped my piece up along my stomach. It pulsated against my navel. Rayven stuck her hand between us and squeezed it. "Dang, you're always riling me up. You ain't right." She breathed heavily and kissed my lips again.

My mother held up her left hand. "Look, y'all need to go get ahold of yourselves. I need to get me some rest anyway. Give me my hugs, and then be on your way," she ordered, sliding under her covers. She grabbed her stocking cap off her tray table, and placed it on her head. Smoothed it down, and laid her head on her pillow.

Rayven slid on the bed next to her, and hugged her body. "Mama, I'ma try and make sure I come up with something every week for you. This time it's a grand, next time it may only be a few hundred, but I'm going to make sure it's something. I love you so much." She closed her eyes and hugged her tight. My mother smiled, then kissed her on both cheeks again. She ran her fingers through her hair.

"I don't know when my son gon' get his stuff together so he can put a ring on your finger. You deserve to be his wife, and he deserve to be your husband. I see so much promise in the two of you. You're both my babies, and I know I will never love any woman he brings home as much as I love you." Her eyes got big. She coughed, and then tried to throw the sheets back so she could get out of the bed. Her left foot got caught. She fell out of the bed to her knees, and threw up all over the floor, coughing the whole way. I rushed to her side, waited until she was finished and picked her up. Took a warm towel and wiped her mouth with it, before kissing her forehead.

"It's okay, beautiful, I'll clean it up. You just try and get some sleep. You need your strength. Do you understand me?" I rubbed her shoulder, and kissed her cheek. She nodded her head with her eyes closed. Her skin was becoming really pale. She shook as if it was below zero in the room. Rayven went into action, cleaning up the mess my mother had made.

"Mama, I love you so much and I know you're going to fight through this. I want you to know we're going to be with you every step of the way. You're not alone." She began to mop up the mess with her eyes tearing up.

"Thank you, baby. That makes me feel so good," my mother said, shivering like crazy. I placed the sheets fully over her body, then got up and grabbed a blanket from the couch and placed that over her as well. After it was in place, I rested my cheek against hers and rocked her to sleep. Rayven climbed in the bed on the other side of her, and laid her head on my mother's shoulder. Clasping her fingers into her own, she kissed the back of her hand over and over.

"You think she's going to be okay, Kaleb?" She wiped away a tear. I took a deep breath, and kissed the side of my mother's forehead.

"Yeah, she's a fighter. This is a warrior right here. I've never known her to lose a battle. She's had this cancer for two years and it ain't took her out yet, and it never will. The doctors say the chemotherapy should get rid of it altogether. I just gotta make sure I keep coming through every week with her payments. It's hard, but I'll do anything for this goddess right here." I laid my cheek on hers again.

"I swear I'll do all that I can, Kaleb. Maybe I should start taking some of those tricks up on their offers. I mean, especially if it can help her." Her voice was starting to break up. I could tell she was getting emotional.

"Nall, ma, don't belittle yourself like that. I got her. I know what I gotta do. I just gotta go out and do it. I'll never

24

fail my world right here. This my baby. I'ma make sure she has everything she needs." Rayven shook her head.

"Nall, Kaleb. That's not how it's supposed to be. Now, I know that she's not my biological mother, but I love her as if she is. She's my heart just as much as she is yours, and she's always been there for me for as long as I've known her. I'm not going to let you figure things out on your own. I don't know what I'm going to do yet, but I am going to help you meet that quota every week. I promise you that." She cuddled up next to my mother, and laid her head on her shoulder, kissing her cheek, then looking over at me. The nurse knocked on the door twice, then stepped into the room with a clipboard in her hand. She looked over at my sleeping mother and smiled, tapping her wrist watch, indicating visiting hours were over for the day.

T.J. Edwards

Chapter 3

I grabbed Rayven's wrist and tried to pull her into my place. She pulled back, and shook her head. "Nall, Kaleb, I'm tired. Besides, I got a lot on my mind. Just give me a hug, and I'll see you in the morning. Tomorrow is another day." I pulled her more firmly to my chest, reached around and cuffed that ass, rubbing all over it. The globes felt soft and warm.

"Baby, stop playing with me. I need some of you tonight, and you're right, tomorrow is another day. Now, bring yo ass in here and give me what I want." I sucked her neck and licked along the length of it. She tasted as good as she looked.

"Stop, baby. I gotta be at the club later on tonight. I don't want to be all tired and shit. You're going to make me tired all night," she said, trying to pry herself away from me.

I squeezed that ass and picked her up. She wrapped her legs around my body and moaned in my ear. "Yo, you know how I get down. I ain't asking you no more. Don't make me take this pussy." I carried her into my apartment and kicked the door closed behind me.

"That's what you gon' have to do, because ain't nothing happening, Kaleb. I told you I don't feel like it right now. I gotta go to work later." She jumped out of my embrace and tried to push me aside. Made a dash for the door, got it part way opened, before I slammed it back and locked it. She went for it again. "Move out of my way and stop playing wit me." I pulled her thick ass to me, wrapped my arms around her body, and fell to the floor with her.

"You know I ain't got no problem taking this shit." I yanked open her jean jacket, and pulled her blouse up over her bra, before ripping it. Her breasts spilled out into the open. I cupped them and sucked first the right nipple into my mouth, twirling my tongue all around it.

She fought against me to free herself, popping her hips, trying to hump me up off of her. "Get off me, Kaleb. Stop, please. I'm not playin wit you." I twirled my tongue around the next nipple. Sucked it into my mouth and pulled hard, while my fingers worked at the buttons on her jeans. Once I had them open, I yanked the pants down her thick thighs. It was a task, but I made it happen. They got as low as her calf muscles, before my face was in between her legs, licking up and down her bald slit. She was without panties. Her kitty was already dripping its essence. It was savory on my tongue. Her knees were pushed to her breasts.

"Kaleb. Kaleb, stop. Un! Please, stop. Oh, my God. Un!" she moaned, and closed her eyes tight, her body shaking already. I peeled the lips apart, and attacked her clitoris with my tongue, flicking it over and over again, before sucking it into my lips, and swallowing the juices that came out of her hole. My tongue reached as far into her as it could go, sliding in and out. My nose and chin were greasy with her fluids. She dug her nails into the carpet. "You're always doing me like this. You're always taking this pussy. Oh, my God, Kaleb. Why?" I nipped at her clit with my teeth, then slurped it into my lips again. This caused her to shiver and buck into my face. All I had to do was make her cum. Whenever I snatched Rayven up and took her kitty, as long as I made her cum during the process, it turned her into an animal. Her inner ho came out. I needed her. I wanted her body in the worst way.

Needed it to take my mind off of my mother, and what had taken place with Buddy. I stuck my head up. "Cum in my mouth, Rayven. Gimme that shit. Cum all in daddy mouth, baby. Now!" I slid two fingers into her pussy and sucked on the top of her cat again, flicking my tongue back and forth across it, pushing her knees further into her chest.

"Shut up, Kaleb! Shut up! Oh my God! I'm cumming. You son of a bitch! I'm cumming. I hate you!" she screamed. Sat all the way up and came hard. Shaking and screaming. She cupped her titties and pulled on the long brown nipples. Sweat slid down the side of her face. I sucked all over her thighs, cleaning up the mess of her essence, not wanting to miss a single drip of it. Then, I sat back on my knees and pulled my piece out of my jeans, stroking it up and down. Feeling the thick veins pulsate under my fingers.

"Come suck on me, ma. Come on, baby. I need to feel that heat right now," I said, looking between her legs at her fat pussy lips. They were slightly separated, just enough for me to see her inner pink. A clear string of juice leaked out of her, and slid over her ass cheeks. It looked so good to me, and reminded me of the first time I'd eaten her kitty when we were only twelve years old. "Come on, baby. Don't leave me like this." She laid on her back and slid her hands between her legs. Opened her pussy lips wide, and sucked on her bottom lip.

"You remember you used to make me play wit myself and watch you do that when we were little?" she asked, rolling her middle finger around her clit, taking the time out to suck her juices off of it every so often. I watched her tongue lick it up and down. I shuddered. "Yeah, baby. That's because you was scared for me to put all of this in you back then."

"You used to have to work yourself up first." I stroked my piece faster, watching her play with herself. Taking me back to when we were kids. She pulled her jeans off, and threw then to the side of her. Placed her feet on the carpet, and spread her thighs wide. Her fingers played over her sex.

"You always made me so wet. My little panties used to stick to me. I didn't even know what was happening to me most of the time. My little kitty was on fire, just like it is right now. Oh, you drove me so crazy. You made me a fast little girl. Even when you wasn't around me, I used to finger myself, thinking about how your thing looked the last time I saw it. My mother almost caught me a few times doing it." She opened her sex lips wide, showing me her tiny hole. It looked silky as the insides of a rose.

"Rayven, I'll take that shit just like I did back then. Stop playing wit me. Come over here and get me right, ma. Fa real." I was so horny, I was squeezing my dick in my hand as if I was choking it. The head was a bright reddish purple. There were veins all over it. It jumped in my hand.

Rayven got on her knees, turned her back to me, and laid her face on the carpet. Her ass was stuck in the air. Juices poured out of her kitty, down her thick thighs. "You remember that you used to make me do this pose, while you stroked your thing to me? My mother was in the other room and didn't even know what we were doing. I was only twelve and ready for whatever. The only thing I was scared of was getting pregnant." She slid her middle finger into herself, and slowly began to twerk on it. Spread her knees, and really got to riding the digit. Every time the finger left her hole, it was shinier than before. I could really smell her scent now and it was getting to me. "Come on, Kaleb. Take it like you did back then. Let's be twelve again. I'm scared. If you want it, take it." She placed her open palms on the carpet, and made her ass pop up and down. Her pussy slapped the carpet again and again. I rushed behind her, and grabbed ahold of her hips. Stuck my face into her crack, licking up and down in between her ass cheeks. My tongue swiped at her rose bud, before I slid my tongue into it.

Fucking it in and out, ventured down, and slurped her entire sex into my mouth.

"Un! Kaleb, what are you waiting on? Come take my pussy, daddy. Please. I need you to take it, and fuck me hard. I need all of that piece in me," she groaned, spreading her knees further. I stuck my nose into her pussy hole and sniffed as hard as I could, just like I used to when we were on the school bus and she was scared to let me finger it, so I'd be reduced to sniffing and licking her while she squeezed my penis in her little hand.

I got up, and grabbed a handful of her hair. "Suck this dick, ma. Now." I placed the helmet on to her juicy lips. "Taste daddy."

She swiped at me with her tongue, then nudged her head forward to get it. "Closer, daddy. Closer. I wanna taste you now. Please." I walked forward on my knees. She grasped me in her little fist and brought my head to her mouth. Sucking me in. "Daddy," she said, talking with my tool in her mouth.

"Um." I closed my eyes as the heat enveloped me. Her thick lips were like vice grips. She came to her knees, and began to spear her head in my lap, making loud sucking noises. I shivered, and tightened my fingers in her hair, loving the feel of her. "Baby, I'm already close. I'm about to cum already, ma. This head one-hunnit, boo. This head one-hunnit." I closed my eyes tight and pumped my hips faster and faster. Her sucking became fierce. Moaning around the tool in her mouth, she wrapped her left hand around it, and pulled it back and forth as fast as she could. I opened my eyes in time to see her big titties wobbling on her chest. I took ahold of her right ass cheek and squeezed it, before cumming hard. "Uh, shit, boo. You got me."

"Um." she continued to suck, taking me deeper in her throat while her fist pumped me. I fell to my knees, and wound up on my back with her sucking away at me. She didn't pull away until I was harder than before. Then she popped me out of her mouth and laid a kiss right on the tip of my head, before holding the stalk and straddling me, guiding my tower into her hot, wet, oozing pussy. I felt the head slip through her vagina lips, into her silky oven. It felt like a hot, mushy sponge.

"Un, daddy. Let me ride this dick like you taught me." She leaned forward, placed both of her hands on my chest, and slowly rotated her hips. Her titties shook on her chest. The brown nipples stood up an inch. Her areolas looked swollen and shiny from my spit. "Yes. Yes. Yes. Daddy. Uh. Kaleb. This dick still so big for me. It feel so good though." I took ahold of her ass and palmed it, forcing her to take me deep. Sucked her nipple into my mouth and pulled on it.

"Come on, ma. Come on. Ride me. Ride daddy, baby."

I forced her to go faster and faster until she was bouncing up and down in my lap, whimpering. Sweat dripped off her chin. Some of it appeared in between her breasts, causing them to glisten. She looked so sexy making her sex faces, and gritting her teeth. "Daddy, daddy. Uh. Shit. Yes. Um. I'm about. I'm about to. I'm about to ride this dick all night. I swear." She placed her elbows on each side of me and got to popping her ass as if she were in a strip club. It felt so good, I started to make noises that embarrassed me. Her tongue licked the side of my neck, before biting into it. Her big ass continued to shake as she called herself fucking me with everything that she had. I slid my hand in between her ass crack, and wormed my middle finger into her anus, running it in and out, poking.

"Uh! Kaleb. Get that out of there! Get it out of there, baby! I'm finna cum. I'm finna cum!" she screamed, bit into my neck and started to twerk as fast as she could. Slurping sounds from our sexes resonated in the room. She shivered and came all over me, digging her nails into my chest. I could feel her essence pouring all down my ass crack. We got up and I bent her over the cushions of the couch, slid into her from the back, long stroking that pussy while she dug her face into the pillows, screaming.

"Yeah. Yeah. Yeah, ma. Damn. This pussy fire. It's fire. Fuck, ma." *Bam. Bam. Bam. Bam. Bam.* In and out, beating it harder and harder. It seemed like the harder I hit it, the wetter she became, until she was squirtin' all over me. I held her hips and continued to pound that cat.

"Daddy, daddy. Wait. Fuck. Slow down. Slow down. Un. You killing me. You're killing me. Shit! I'm cumming!" She bit into the cushions and screamed at the top of her lungs, bouncing back into my lap harder and harder. Her ass jiggled. Her thighs shook. Her titties bounced back and forth on her chest. I reached under and took ahold of them. The nipples poked through the spaces of my fingers. The breasts were heavy in my hands. "Yes, daddy. Un! Cum in me! Cum in me! Un! I need to feel you buss in my pussy. Now!" She slammed back into my lap faster and harder. Her head tilted, facing the ceiling. A trace of drool spilled out of the corner of her mouth. I smacked her on the ass and squeezed it, stabbed deeper, as my eyes rolled into the back of my head. I felt her walls squeezing at me. She reached under herself and pinched her clit.

Yelped and it became too much for me. I grabbed a handful of her long hair, and pulled that shit. Smacked her ass five hard times and pushed her into the couch, while I bussed my nut deep in her hot pocket. Jerking like I was having a seizure. I stayed on top of her, buried to the hilt for two minutes. Slid out, and she took ahold of my pipe, and sucked it into her mouth, deep throating her juices off of him, licking all around the head, while looking into my eyes. "Um, was it good for you, daddy?" she asked, popping me out, only to suck me back in after she completed her question. I nodded as she lifted my dick, and pressed the head against my stomach. She sucked first one ball into her mouth and then the other, licking in between the cracks of my legs.

* * *

After we showered, we sat in my bed with big bowls of Cinnamon Toast Crunch cereal, watching television. Rayven laid her head up against my chest. I could smell the shampoo and conditioner she'd used to wash her head. She smelled clean and feminine. Her heat made me feel some type of way. I couldn't deny the feelings I had for her. Feelings I rarely ever expressed to her. She turned to face me after the talk show we were watching went to commercial. Took her thumb, and wiped away a trace of milk in the corner of my mouth. After cleaning it away, she sucked the thumb, and smiled at me. "Kaleb, I don't think I'll ever be able to get you out of my system. I been in love with you since I was twelve. You be driving me all kinds of crazy and stuff. Dang, that's irritating." She continued to look me over.

I took another spoonful of my cereal, and started to crunch on it. Looked down at her, and frowned. "What's good?"

"Dam, I just told you that I love you and you ain't say nothing?"

"Aw, I was wondering why you were looking all crazy and shit." I took another spoonful of cereal and ate it. Chewing wit my eyes closed. When I opened them again, she was mugging me. "What?"

"Boy, I know that ain't all you got to say. You better come better than that after you just climbed from between my legs, especially after I told you no." She sat her bowl on the night table and adjusted herself so she was resting on her right elbow. Her thick left thigh was draped around my waist. I could feel the heat of her garden on my hip. "I'm still crazy about you too. You know that will never change. I just got so much stuff on my mind. I gotta make sure my mother is good. I be feeling less than a man, when I can't see for sure how I'm going to come up with this next four gees. I still gotta get clothes and shoes for my little brother and sister. It's getting colder and colder in New York. I feel swamped, Rayven, but I do love you, though. You know that, right?" I kissed her on the forehead, and gripped her ass, pulling her all the way on top of me.

She sat up, and looked down into my face, concerned. "You know I'm gonna assist you, Kaleb. If you want, I'll take Destiny shopping with me, and you can just take care of Derez. That way, we'll split the work load in half. Then, when it comes to Mama, I'll try and come up with at least two gees before Thursdays. I mean, I really don't wanna imagine giving in to one of these tricks, but if that's what it takes, then it is what it is." She exhaled, then laid her head on my chest.

I rubbed her big booty. Her kitty lips opened up, and were planted against my waistline. I could feel her heat searing me. It caused my penis to slowly rise. "Ma, I don't want you getting down like that. I'll figure it out. Just do what you can for Destiny, and I'll appreciate that. Yo, I'ma make sure I reimburse you too, goddess, because this ain't your burden to be taking on. This why you're my heart though." I hugged her firmly to my body and kissed her soft lips. In my opinion, there was no woman like Rayven. She was so one hunnit, it was hard to not fall in mad love with her. She had the scruples of a queen. A queen that most men like me daydreamed about. I didn't know how I was going to make it happen for my mother, my siblings, and Rayven I knew she would need to lean on me eventually, but I just knew that everything would fall into place when it was supposed to. I just had to keep on praying, and finding a way to master the slums.

Chapter 4

"Son, I never thought I'd see the day where I had to rock a hook on the end of my wrist. I feel like a fucking pirate," Buddy said, taking a huge hit off of the Dutch cigar in his mouth. He blew the smoke out of his nose and shook his head. I sat across from him inside his living room. Took two Percocet pills, and tossed them into my mouth, swallowing and chasing them with Apple juice.

"Son was out of order for cutting ya shit off, when it was clear neither one of us had anything to do with hitting him for that petty change. You got my condolences, kid. I mean that." Buddy waved me off. He pulled a Glock off his waist, and held it in his right hand.

"Long as I can do this." He cocked it with his hook and smiled. "Nigga, I'm good. I'll still buck a nigga ass down. Fuck that hand. I'll make do with what I got."

He replaced the gun, just as his three-year-old daughter came into the living room and climbed on the couch, and into his arms. He hugged, and then kissed her lips. "Hey, baby. You just woke up?" In response, she yawned and closed her eyes again, smacking her little lips together, and falling back to sleep in his arms. "Yo, I'll tell you something else. That fool Sheek gon' pay for this hand, Blood. Mark my words on that. I can't accept this. I'ma lay back in the cut until the timing is right, and then I'ma buck that nigga down, Kid. Son got me walking around looking like a Halloween figure and shit." He patted his daughter on the butt and stood up. "Hold on, kid, let me take her in the back to her mother, then we can head out."

I took the blunt, and took four deep pulls off of it. I was feeling like shit, knowing that I was the reason my man's hand had been cut off. I didn't know how I was going to pay him back for the loss of it. I would have to figure it out like I would everything else. I knew I was bogus, and in many eyes probably even a snake, but I would do anything for my mother. I didn't care what that anything meant. Buddy came back into the living room, zipping up his leather Avirex jacket~ "Yo, let's hit the pavement, kid. Shorty about to get on my nerves and I ain't got time for that shit. Word up." He rolled his eyes and made sure that the handles of his guns weren't showing. His baby mother, Bree, came from the back of the house with an angry scowl on her face. She was dressed in some tight white biker shorts that were molded to her cat. Her chocolate thighs were on full display. She wore a cut-off Von Dutch shirt that displayed her belly ring.

She had been my third grade girlfriend back in the day, and even after the birth of Buddy's daughter, Bree was a sight to see. I couldn't take my eyes off of her crotch because I could see her kitty lips through them. "That's your problem, Buddy. You never want to sit down and talk about anything. You're so quick to run into the streets with our problems on your mind. I'm tired of it." Buddy turned around to face her.

"Shorty, take ya ass back in the room. Now. I'm not playing either," he ordered, pointing. She smacked her lips.

"Fuck that. I'm not scared of you. You need to come back here so we can talk about these finances. We're drowning, and since you're refusing to work, I don't know what to do." She crossed her arms in front of her chest. "Hi, Kaleb, sorry I didn't speak earlier." Her eyes locked into mine. She had a few stretch marks spread over her stomach muscles, which were prominent. Her thighs were shining as if she'd just rubbed baby oil into them. She looked good.

I smiled. "What's good, Bree?" My eyes looked her up and down again. Buddy stepped into her face.

"Bitch, I'm not playing. Get yo punk ass back in that room, or so help me God," he began, his fist balled up. His nostrils flared. Bree looked up at him and frowned.

"Like I said, Buddy. You need to bring your ass back here, so we can talk about these finances. We're about to be kicked out and on the streets. We need to come up with a solution. Now, bring your—" *Smack!*

"Bitch, I told you to take your punk ass back to that room!" he hollered, smacking her so hard that she fell to the floor, holding her face. He grabbed her by the hair and dragged her across the carpet, while she kicked her legs wildly.

"Let me go, Buddy. Let me go. I'm so tired of you beating on me for no reason. This ain't right!" she cried. I reluctantly turned my back on the entire scene, because it was so hard for me to not step in and pull him away from her. I didn't think a man should beat a woman for no reason at all. Seeing him smack her to the floor, with their child in the other room, made me want to get up and knock his ass out. I heard more fighting, slapping, and tussling in the back of the house. Then, their three-year-old was crying loudly. I lowered my head and prayed that Buddy hurried up. I needed to get out of their crib before I intervened. Buddy appeared five minutes later, with a long scratch on the side of his face. Both Bree and their daughter, Breeyonna, were crying in the back room loudly.

"Yo, let's get the fuck out of here, kid. Both of their asses is driving me crazy. Straight up. Give the god two of them pills. My wrist is killing me."

* * *

I scratched the back of my neck, and rolled my head around on my shoulders. I felt hot, and Sheek's basement was both stuffy and smelled stale. I was sitting at a round table located in the middle of the basement. Around it sat me, Buddy, and two other Blood niggas. Sheek came down the stairs, and set a green crate on the top of the table that had U.S. Military printed on the side of it. He took the top of the lid off and pulled an AR-33 out of it. Took one of the fifty round clips, and slammed it into the body of the fully automatic machine gun. "Check out my new toys, fellas. These bitches spit three rapid bullets at a time, and are more accurate than a thirty-thirty hunting rifle. You can count the freckles on a muhfucka's face with this scope from two blocks away. These bitches are going to be the reason we fully take over Harlem. Mark my words on that." He ran his tongue across his teeth, and looked over the four of us. "But, there is only one problem. I got one crate sitting here in front of me, when I should have ten of them."

A chill ran down my spine. I was praying this nigga wasn't saying that somebody had stolen the other crates and we were the ones he thought had something to do with it. I didn't have time to be going through a bunch of nonsense. I had two days until my mother had to have another four gees to pay for her treatments. The last thing I needed was to be beefing with Sheek and his thugs. "Son, so what are you saying? Are you saying you think somebody in this room stole ya shit?" I asked, getting irritated. He snickered, and aimed the gun at each member sitting at the table, ending with the barrel aimed at me.

"Lil nigga, if I thought anything like that, I wouldn't be talking, I'd be shooting right now." He curled his upper lip. Tapped the trigger and a red beam appeared on my forehead. I got vexed, stood up and knocked the barrel out of my face.

"Get that shit out of my face, nigga. That ain't cool," I snapped.

My chest rose and fell. I didn't give a fuck how many men followed behind this nigga. I wasn't about to let him treat me like a bitch under no circumstances. That shit wasn't in me. He took a step back and pointed the gun at me again. "Nigga, if you don't sit yo ass down, I'ma blow ya fucking head off. That's on my Blood," he swore, his eyes brows turned downward. I pulled my pistol off my hip and cocked it. Aimed it at him.

"Yo, I don't know why you think it's sweet, but ain't no hoes over here. If you gon' stank me, Blood, you going wit me. That's on my mother." Buddy scooted his seat back and took the Glock off his waist.

"Say, Slime. cut that bullshit out. My mans was sitting here mindin' his business, you ain't have no right pointing that shit in his face. How else do you expect him to react?" Buddy asked, cocking his Glock, ready for whatever. Sheek laughed to himself and turned the barrel on Buddy.

"Oh, you tough too, then? Aight, let's see how tough you niggas are then." He lowered the AR-33 and smiled. "I got a mission for you niggas." He tossed the AR-33 to me, and I caught it with one hand, looking it over. "Like I said, there are nine more crates out there. Nine more that needs to be brought to the mob. We need to snatch up these crates before our foes get their hands on them. Once they are obtained, then we can start to bully shit and get the funds that will help all of us to live a little better. I know you niggas tired of barely getting by. Well, in order to make the money, we need the power. Our power will come from these firearms." He said this, walking around the table. He stopped and placed his hand on my shoulder. I felt like pushing his shit off of me. I didn't like no man touching me, period. I felt awkward.

"Yo, all that shit sound good for the long haul, but what about today, son? I need scratch today. I got priorities at home, and so does the god over there." I nodded my head at Buddy. Sheek stepped away from me and turned his back. "How much bread you talking, money?" There was a pitbull chained to the water heater in the corner of the basement. He walked over to it, and took his chains from around the pipes. Wrapped the chain around his hand a few times, then stepped over to the round table. I rested my hand on the handle of my gun. If that dog moved in the slightest, I was going to buck his ass down. I hated pits. They couldn't be trusted. I'd seen more than one turn on their master, and attack him. So, I was leery and ready.

"I personally need about four bands. But, that's just speaking for me. I don't know how much my mans need." I turned to stare at Buddy.

"That amount sound good to me. So, I guess we thinking eight stacks. You got something lined up that a gross that?" Buddy asked, looking over the AR-33 I'd handed to him.

Sheek nodded. "Yep, but you niggas gon' have to get your hands dirty, and not ask any questions. Shit can get bloody too. I'm talking real bloody." He looked into my eyes, and then over to Buddy.

"Yo, I'm down for whatever long as it make them chips add up. The god got obligations." Buddy aimed the AR-33 at the wall, after enacting the red beam on the top of it.

"What about you, Kaleb? You down for whatever too?" Sheek asked, taking a Newport Short out of his pocket and placing it into his lips. He took his lighter and set fire to it. All I could see was my mother laying in the hospital bed, struggling to make it through each day. I couldn't fail her. I had to make sure that she had everything that she needed. It was my duty to. She was my queen. I couldn't fail her.

"Yo, count me in. Long as I can come away with at least four gees for myself, I'm wit it." Sheek nodded.

"Yeah, aight. I'ma hit your phone first thing in the morning at about five. Be ready to roll out. I'ma pay you up front for what I'ma have you do. Matter fact." He loosened his belt and dug his hand in between his legs. Came up with a knot of hundreds. Took the rubber band off the knot and counted out forty, one-hundred-dollar bills, handed them to me, then did the same to Buddy. "Huh. That's four apiece. Y'all go do what you have to. But, make sure you're ready to go first thing in the morning, no questions asked."

* * *

An hour later, me and Buddy were walking down Times Square. It was a little after nine at night, and I needed to clear my head. Snow fell from the sky in patches. Though it was snowing, it wasn't that cold to me. "Yo, why every time you say you need to think, we wind up in Times Square, kid?" Buddy popped his collar, and blew into his gloved hands. Some of his smoke from the cold wafted over to me. It smelled like onions. I held my breath for a second. I looked up at one of the digital billboards that advertised all the attractions set to come to New York this winter.

"Kid, I come down here to remind myself that life is bigger than New York. I don't wanna be stuck in the slums my whole life, son. Harlem ain't what's good, Blood. I want outta here. I wanna be somebody major one day."

The wind blew and sent a flurry of snow into my ear canal. I brushed it out, then pulled my skull cap further down. Buddy walked over and looked up at the marquee that promoted the game between the New York Knicks and the Los Angeles Lakers. "They got Lebron coming to town, kid. Yo, I gotta go to that game. Son only got a few years in the league. I gotta see him play up close and personal, Dunn.

It's a dream of mine." He nodded his head with a smile on his face. I looked up, and read the marquee.

"We'll go. I'll make sure you have those tickets." The game was set for a week before Christmas. I had to get my hands on those tickets. "Yo, did you see how that nigga pulled out a knot of hundreds, then handed us eight bands like it wasn't nothing?" I asked, looking over at Buddy. People continued to walk past us. Every now and then, somebody would brush up against me and keep walking.

The streets were crowded. They were always crowded in Times Square. Buddy shrugged his shoulders and started to walk down the block. "So what? He should have chips like that. He got a bunch of us working under him. What did you expect?"

"That's what I'm saying. Kid got all that bread, because we hit the streets and do all of the dirty work for him. We're chasing his bag and all he gotta do is sit back and collect the profits. We just took a job for eight gees. Eight gees that he peeled off like it wasn't nothing. And we don't even know what the job is." I was having second thoughts. The whole scene was replaying itself in my mind now. I felt like Sheek had a bunch of bullshit up his sleeve, and he was about to put us on the front lines of it.

"Long as I got my paper, I don't give a fuck. I'm tired of Bree riding me. We got so many bills, I feel like I'm drowning, kid. Every day, I wanna pull a ho move and never return home. My father did it to us, and I ain't heard from that nigga since. He probably got tired of the responsibilities that come along with having a family. It sucks at times." I stopped midstride, mugged him.

"Yo, I swear, if I ever hear you talk like a pussy again, I'ma take yo head off. Only pussies run out on their women after the child comes. Just because you run off, don't mean that Bree and Breeyonna's struggles stop. You're supposed to be their protector, their shield from this cold world. If their shield is gone, then they are vulnerable to everything because you chose to expose their vulnerabilities. That makes you a bitch, and not a man. I'd rather die on my two feet fighting for my family, then to run off like a wimp. A man faces each battle head on and acts as a sacrifice for those in his domain, not the contrary. You gotta fight, even if it kills you." He nodded and smiled, while looking at the ground.

"Damn, son. Why you so passionate about all of that? I was just telling you how I was feeling. Not that I was going to run away or nothin' like that. Bree do get on my nerves though. I got this young side bitch that don't give me no problems at all. She calling me daddy and everything. She ain't even sweating the missing hand. I be wanting to stay shacked up wit her all day, and just start from scratch with a new Earth. Word is bond. She got the kid nose wide open. Not on no love shit, but you know."

"Nigga, all I know is that you better get Bree and your family right first. You can have your lil side piece if that's what you want, but the mother of your child and your child, has to come first. Word up. I'll buss ya ass if they don't. Come on."

T.J. Edwards

Chapter 5

The next morning, Sheek hit me up at four-thirty on bidness. I snatched up Buddy, and we met up with Sheek and two of his home boys outside Yonkers, New York. I had a migraine that was killing me so bad, my vision was going blurry. I felt sick and my mouth was dry, even though I was sipping on a bottle of orange juice. Earlier that night, I'd gotten a call from Rayven, saying that she wanted us to have lunch at one in the afternoon. She wanted to run something by me that was important, and she wouldn't tell me what it was. So, I had that on my mind, and my mother. She'd come down with pneumonia out of the blue and I was worried about her immune system not being able to fight off the sickness, because her T-cell count was so low.

I pulled into the back of an aluminum warehouse, where Sheek and his men were already parked at the ready. When I pulled in back of their van, he got out of the passenger's seat and walked to the back of my Monte Carlo. Opened the back door, and sat down. "Yo, what's good, gods?" he asked, shaking up with me and then Buddy. I nodded, and turned to face him.

"What's on the agenda?" He had yet to tell us what we'd be doing. I was still a bit leery because I didn't trust him, or no man for that matter. Not even Buddy. I felt that in time, the karma of his hand situation would come to the forefront and clap back at me. So, I kept my eyes peeled for any sight of shiesty when it came to him.

"Jamaicans. In order for me to get that nine crates of firepower we need, we gotta stop a boat full of Jamaicans that's set to come through the harbor in about an hour. My connect say he want the whole boat massacred."

He ran a finger across his throat, and closed his eyes to emphasize his point. Buddy nodded. "Yo, we killing dread heads? Shit, I'm wit it. The first time I got shot was by a Jamaican bitch. Shorty tried to end the kid, but real niggas don't die. Nah' mean?" I mugged him from the corners of my eye, and wanted to tell him to shut the fuck up. It seemed like he never saw the bigger picture. He only looked on the surface of things and that could be deadly.

"Yo, if we're hitting up a ship full of dread heads that means somebody got a vendetta against them, or whoever is sending them over. Now on the one hand, if we annihilate them, we're advancing your status and getting the weapons that we need to go at the city hard. But on the other hand, these dread heads belong to somebody. We'll be crossing them and asking for a war with whoever they belong to. Are you willing to endure that? For a punk ass four gees, Buddy?" I mugged Sheek while I awaited the answer from Buddy. He shook his head.

"Nall, nigga, it don't go like that. Y'all already took my money for a blind mission. Once you left my basement with that cash, it put this move in play. This is what it is, point blank. So, ain't no reason to ask Buddy how he feeling. Get ready to handle this bidness and we'll go from there. You got that?" he snapped, with spit flying from his mouth.

The car was quiet for a long time. I sat looking at my lap. My nostrils flared. My heart beat so hard in my chest that I could hear it in my ears. I wanted to go berserk. To turn around and put two in Sheek's face. But, killing him meant I would have every Blood in Harlem at my ass. That was drama I didn't need. Plus, most of the mob knew where my brother and sister laid their heads. It was dangerous. I had fucked up by taking the money. I should have been less anxious, and more conscious of the situation. It was a lesson to be learned. I'd have to take this hit on the chin. "Aight, Sheek. Lead the way, Dunn. Me and Buddy a follow you."

"When we get to the docks, there is going to be an older Jamaican woman with gray dreadlocks. She's going to give us a boat and when she does, we're going to get on that boat and meet these dread heads about three hunnit meters out, slay the whole ship, and keep it moving. Wet everything. This is a kill mission. Do I make myself clear?" Though he was asking this question of both of us, he was only staring at me. I nodded my head.

"Yeah, money, it's good. Like I said, lead the way and me and my mans gon' follow you."

"Yeah, aight, stay close behind and don't be driving all crazy and shit." He stepped out of the whip and slammed the door. Mugged me through the window and shook his head. He walked away, mumbling to himself.

"Yo, I swear to God, son, I'ma stank that nigga one day. I hate that nigga wit a passion kid, straight up," Buddy said, mugging the back of Sheek's head, before he disappeared into the whip that he and his crew came in. I was too busy wondering why Sheek wanted us along for the mission, since he had so many other niggas at his disposal.

Something wasn't adding up in my book. I hated when I couldn't figure something out that was nagging at me. I didn't trust Sheek, or neither one of them other niggas that ran under him either. I needed to break away from the Bloods in general. I wanted to be my own king. An army of one, I didn't need a whole bunch of niggas to validate me or my manhood.

"Did you hear what I said, Kaleb? I wanna stank that nigga."

"Yeah I heard you, B., but now ain't the time to think about all of that. We gotta stay focused on the task at hand. Nah' mean?" He nodded, still mugging Sheek's whip.

"Yeah, I hear you, kid. I'm just waiting on my moment though. Sooner or later, a muhfucka gon' have to pay for this nub. You'll see."

I felt a twinge of guilt travel through me as I looked down to the portion of his wrist where his hand used to be. I still felt horrible about that whole debacle, but there wasn't nothing that I could do about it right then. "We'll get 'em, kid. Trust me on that. When the time is right, we'll get him."

* * *

I tucked the bottom portion of my mask into the collar of my black hoodie, and pulled the hood over my face. The wind coming off the harbor was fierce. So harsh that I could barely keep my eyes opened. On top of that, I was freezing. My teeth chattered together. I could feel chill bumps all over me. My nose was so cold, it was making my head hurt. I was wishing I had dressed more appropriately for the weather, but I was so used to hitting licks in my hoodie that I'd gotten lost in the sauce. I jumped off the dock and into the boat. As soon as my feet hit the deck, Sheek gave me one of those half-hugs that were passed out in the hood, when you wanted to show your love and respect to a comrade.

I took it, but cringed throughout the process. Son smelled real musty, like he hadn't taken a shower in a few days or something. I hated the smell of men. "Yo, I'm counting on you to do your thing, Kaleb. I know underneath it all, you got that killer shit in you. I see it when I look into your eyes, lil homie. Let them pistols buss until they're empty, and fall back. You feel me?" A draft of wind came through and blew my hood off my head, leaving my neck exposed to the cold air. Before I could respond to him, hail began to come down from the sky, and it turned pitch black all of a sudden.

"I'ma handle my bidness, Blood, you ain't gotta worry about that. Let's get this show on the road." I stepped past him and pulled out one .45 and cocked it first, and then its twin. I was ready to smoke some shit and get it over with.

The older Jamaican woman Sheek had been talking about stepped foot onto the boat, looked me up and down, and walked past me. She made her way to the controls of the boat, just as some older Blood niggas gave the boat a push away from the docks. I could hear the motor start. It clicked on with a loud roar. I watched it slowly move out into the harbor. Buddy stood in the middle of the deck with his arms out, looking at the sky.

"Yo, I swear this is murdering weather, B. All of a sudden, when we getting ready to sweat some shit, it gets dark and this happens. What are the odds?" He shook his head and posted up in the center of the boat with the rest of the Bloods. I knelt down just outside of their pack, with my mother on my mind. I was praying that she was feeling better. The doctors had told me that pneumonia spelled trouble for any patient undergoing chemotherapy. That the few white blood cells that she had left weren't exactly strong enough to fight off the sickness. They would be relying on the antibiotics, among a long list of other things. I tried to center myself and expect the best. Rayven had promised to stop in and check on her this morning and I was thankful for that. Thankful for her in general. The boat swayed from side to side. The hail seemed to get worse. It felt like heavy pellets were attacking us from above. The temperature dropped, and now I couldn't feel my fingers inside of the leather gloves that were overrated. I remained on one knee, lost in deep thought until I was disrupted fifteen minutes into our travels.

"Yo niggas, listen up," Sheek said, with smoke from the cold coming out of his mouth. "We about to be pulling up to their boat in less than   five minutes. Everybody get ready. Follow my lead. I'ma kick shit off out of the gate, and we gon' take it from there. Remember what I said, everybody on that boat must die. We ain't sparing nobody. Word up. Get ready." He stepped back into the place where the older Jamaican woman was steering the boat, leaving us to talk among ourselves. I pulled Buddy to the side.

"Say bruh, when we get on there, you watch my back and I'll watch yours. I don't know what this nigga got up his sleeve, and neither do you. So, all we got is each other. Let's go ahead and handle this bidness so we can be on our way. We ain't fucking wit this nigga after this."

"Yeah aight, kid. I'm wit you. Just watch my blind side. You know I'm only fucking wit one hand." He laughed, but I knew he was serious.

I nodded and took a step back, knelt to one knee and said a silent prayer in my head. "Father, please help me to make it through this battle, or whatever it is I'm about to walk into. I ask that You forgive me ahead of time for the lives that I am about to take. Amen." I looked toward the sky, and took a deep breath, breathing it out. Ready to get this shit over with. The sky darkened, and the wind began to whistle loudly. Sheek held up his hand.

"Alright, Slime, here we go. Mask on." The Jamaican woman steered the boat as close as she could to another smaller boat. As soon as she did, there was a heavyset man standing on the dock of the other boat. He wore a black jacket with fur around the hood. His gloves were all white.

He took a long thick rope and tossed it across the water, onto the boat that we were in. Sheek caught the rope and pulled it as hard as he could.

After ten minutes and some maneuvering by the older Jamaican woman, the boats finally came side by side. Sheek tied the rope around a metal anchor to keep it in place. After confirming it was secure, he waved the heavyset man over. Now, the hail had turned into a heavy downpour of cold rain that felt like marbles being cast from the sky. I watched the heavyset man step his black rubber boots onto the deck of our boat. He extended his hand, and walked toward Sheek. "My friend, I'm so glad that you were able to make it on time. I have fifty-eight passengers that need to board this ship. I'll be right back." He made an attempt to step back onto his boat when Sheek grabbed his arm. He yanked it away. "What's the matter, mon?"

"Before anybody come onto this boat, I need to make sure you got my money and my guns."

The heavyset Jamaican frowned. "Of course I got what we agreed upon. Ya don't take me for a snake, do ya now, boy?" He looked over his shoulder back to his boat. "Seven hundred and fifty thousand, and three crates of artillery. As promised. It's in the cabin below the deck, next to the controls. Come on." He waved Sheek to follow him. The old Jamaican woman stepped onto the deck with a weird smile on her face. When the heavyset Jamaican man saw her his eyes got as big as paper plates.

"Now, Sheek. Kill this bumbaclot!" Sheek pulled a .9 millimeter out of his waistband, and pressed it to the heavyset man's cheek before he could reach for his own weapon. He pulled the trigger two quick times. *Boom. Boom.* Fire spit from the gun. The shells popped out of it and landed on the deck of the boat. The heavyset man's face was blown halfway off.

He leaped backward in the air and wound up wedged between the two boats. Smoke from the gun rose in the air and was taken away by the wind, just as lighting flashed overhead. "Let's move. Murder everything moving!" Sheek ordered, hopping over the dead man and waving us to follow him. I was third in line, right behind Buddy, who struggled to climb on to the other boat until I helped him. The rain was coming down so hard it made the deck slippery. It felt like we were walking on ice. Sheek balanced his way to the first red door we saw on the ship, leaned his shoulder against it, then rammed it until it bussed open. The door crashed into the wall behind it, and screams were emitted from the inside. Before I could get up close enough to see what was going on, I heard multiple gunshots from Sheek's weapon. He rushed further into the door, and when I got into the cabin, I saw two females laying on the floor with their brains leaking out of their skulls.

On the side of them were two little boys, both had been gunned down. I frowned, and felt sick. "What the fuck?" More shots erupted from deeper inside of the cabin. The smell of gun smoke and feces rose into the air. I rushed to the next room. The cabin was narrow, and compact. The air was thick. I could barely breathe inside of it. But, I kept on following, trying to catch up with Sheek and Buddy. Along the floor, I found more women and children's bodies. It wasn't until we got to the stairs that led into the bottom of the boat that I understood what this mission was shaping up to be. When I got down into the basement portion of the cabin, I saw about twenty-five Jamaican women, all huddled in a corner of the boat, hugging their children in fear of the unknown. I could hear their whimpering. Their children cried at the top of their lungs.

Sheek slammed a clip into the bottom of his AR-33, and cocked it. "Exterminate these bitches and let's get the fuck out of here." He hollered over his shoulder. I looked at Buddy, and he looked at me. The other two Bloods that had come along for the journey stood beside Sheek, ready to blow the women to dust. They held AR-33's in their hands as well.

"Yo, we about to kill a bunch of women, son?" I hollered with my guns drawn. I was confused. Why the fuck did he need a bunch of us with him to pull off a move on a bunch of defenseless females? I didn't get it, nor was I with this shit. This was fuck shit to me. Sheek mugged me over his shoulder. "Nigga, buss yo guns, now! I ain't gon' say that shit again!" he snapped.

The females started to scream. "Please! Please! Please! Don't do this!" The little kids were crying, with tears running down their cheeks, hugging their mothers. They looked petrified. I imagined them being my little brother and sister, and felt horrible at their predicament. "Please!" a woman screamed. Buddy raised his gun at the women.

"Fuck we gon' do, Kaleb? It's now or never, my nigga." He looked from me to Sheek, and back to me again. I could tell that he was on the verge of panicking. I raised both guns and aimed them at Sheek.

"Blood, I can't let you kill these females, B. Let's just take the money and get the fuck out of here. They're innocent! This shit ain't right! They ain't no threat," I barked, feeling my heart pound in my chest. I couldn't believe I had my gun drawn on him.

No matter what happened now, me and this nigga was about to be beefing until one of us were murdered. That's just how it went in Harlem. "Yo, I'll deal wit you later. Blast these bitches!" He turned back to the women and children, and all three of their assault rifles began to go off at once.

Boom. Boom. Boom. Boom. Boom. The room lit up, shells tinkled on the floor. The women and kids began to scream at the top of their lungs in agony. They shook against the wall before falling to the ground, riddled by bullets. Yet, Sheek and his shooters continued to gun them down as if they were the ultimate enemy. I stood there perplexed, not knowing what to do, or what to say. The shooting went on for two straight minutes, and then it was done. All the victims were sprawled out on the floor, laying in puddles of fresh blood.

After Sheek saw that all of them were annihilated, he turned around to face me and Buddy. "When we get off this boat, I want my muthafuckin' money back. I'll be by to holler at both of you niggas. Now, let's get the fuck out of here. Now!" He brushed past me and bumped my shoulder.

Buddy took two steps to the right and slammed his gun to Sheek's forehead. "Nall, nigga, it ain't going down like that." *Boom.* Sheek's head jerked on his shoulders before it exploded, and he flew backward into his men. Buddy stood over him and emptied the clip of his gun, then began to stomp what was left of his head with the sole of his Timbs.

Sheek's men looked to scramble. I personally knew that their rifles were empty. I'd heard them clicking while they pulled on the triggers to spit more bullets out of their weapons. Before I could even think about it, I turned my guns on them and finger fucked the triggers.

Boom. Boom. Boom. Boom. The bullets slammed into their chests and faces, knocking the life out of them. Buddy tapped me on the back and rushed out of the cabin. "Come on, bruh, let's get that money he was talking about. We rushed to the control room and searched around until we found the crates the heavyset Jamaican was talking about. After getting everything, it took us five more minutes to drag it to the dock. Once there, he helped me to lift it over the lip of the boat, onto the next one, before we climbed onto that one.

The older Jamaican woman appeared with eyes wide open. "What have you done? Where is my nephew? Where is Sheek?" She looked bewildered. I dropped the crate and held up my hands.

"Say, lady, that nigga killed a bunch of females. We wasn't wit that shit. He had to go. All you gotta do is steer this boat back to the docks and leave it at that."

She took out her phone. "Stay back, stay back." As she said this, she walked backwards toward the edge of the boat. Lightning flashed across the sky again. Then, the hail started even harder than before. The old woman took five pictures with her phone, got onto the edge of the boat, looked over her shoulder. "You'll pay for this. You'll pay for this, I swear, you will." She jumped backwards into the water, creating a big splash.

I rushed to the edge of the boat with my gun out. Searching, trying to locate this crazy ass woman. But, no matter where I looked, I couldn't find her. It blew my mind and on top of that, I was paranoid. Buddy came from behind me and placed his hand on my shoulder. "Fuck that old geezer, Blood, let's get the fuck up out of here."

T.J. Edwards

Chapter 6

My head was so fucked up from seeing all of them women being killed that I completely forgot about the meeting with Rayven. I needed to see my mother, so after me and Buddy split the profits and guns down the middle, I headed over to Mount Sinai Hospital and hugged up with my mother. She appeared to be doing a lot better, and I was thankful for that. She slept most of the time, and all of the peace and quiet started to get to me. I kept on thinking about the women, and the two niggas I'd killed. Even though I didn't know them like that, I'd seen them around Harlem more than a hundred plus times. Every time I closed my eyes, I saw the condition I'd left their dead bodies in. I felt like I could smell the scent of their burnt flesh.

It was crazy. I wound up staying in the hospital with my mother for four days straight, until she woke up and was strong enough to hold a conversation with me. This didn't happen until the following Tuesday, after I was finally able to get a few hours of sleep. She woke me up with kisses. I opened my eyes with a frown on my face. "Boy, fix your face. It ain't nobody but me. Why have you been here this long? Have you even checked in on your sister and lil brother?" she asked, digging cold out of my eyes, and wiping it on a Kleenex that was in her hand. I opened my eyes wide, to allow her to do what she was trying to accomplish.

"Yeah, I done been home a few times. Plus, Rayven holding them down. I just been concerned about you, so I had to be here. That's all." I licked my dry lips.

She finished her grooming and kissed my cheeks. "Yeah, I hear what you saying, but that definitely ain't all. How did you manage to pay up my treatments for the rest of this year? Huh? Walmart give you a raise?" She raised her right eyebrow, and sat on the bed beside me. I wrapped my arm around her shoulder and pressed my lips to her forehead.

"Nah, I ain't been to work in nearly two months. Me and Buddy hit a crazy lick that paid off. It's some beef that's about to come along with it, but I'ma stand on my two feet as a man and do what I gotta do in these streets. You're my church and I'll sacrifice anything for you, including my life."

She wiggled out of my embrace and stood in front of me, looked into my eyes with her gray ones that matched my own. Took my hands, and kissed the palms of them. "Baby, I am not your church. I am your mother. The Bible says only a man's wife can be his church. And if you are to sacrifice yourself and your life for anybody, it is not supposed to be anybody other than your wife." She rubbed my cheek with her soft hand. "Do you understand that, my prince?" I shook my head.

"Nall, I get what the Bible say, but my heart say different. My heart say I gotta go to the ends of the earth for you, and I am. You are my everything. You brought me into this world, and you've sacrificed yourself for me and my siblings ever since we've been here. My father was a pussy, Mama. You're the only father I've ever known." I stood up and pulled her into my embrace. "If I won't sacrifice myself for you, then who will?" She looked into my eyes and took a deep breath. Brought her head forward until it was laying on my chest.

"How many had to die for that money, son?" She wrapped her arms around my waist.

"I don't even know the number. I know I personally took two out of the game, but that's just because I didn't agree with how the move went down. The niggas we hit the lick with, killed about twenty females from Jamaica, and almost as many children. I didn't know what the move was until it

60

was too late." I held her tighter. "I feel sick, Mama. I don't even get down like that." I don't know where it came from, but when I closed my eyes, tears sailed down my cheeks. I kept seeing those females' faces after they'd been massacred. And even before, when they were begging for their lives. I was wishing I had stepped in earlier. Maybe I could have prevented their deaths. I didn't have no problem killing up a bunch of armed rivals, but innocent females and kids? Man that was just bogus to me. I wasn't that type of nigga, and never would be.

"Baby, it's not your fault. The game is what it is. I know my son. I know you would never hurt a bunch of women, or children. It's not in your soul to do so." She took a step back and held my face in her small hands. "You are my blessing. My first-born prince. All of the strength that has ever been inside of me is inside of you, and much more. You are a Haitian warrior by blood." She smiled. "There has never been a person that has walked this earth that loves me as much as you do. You make me so happy. You were worth the stretch marks." She laughed, and hugged my body. "Son, I don't have much longer on this earth. They are doing all they can, but my time is running out. I need for you to stop fighting for me so hard and to begin to focus on the wellbeing of Destiny and Derez. Their futures can only be as bright as you fight for them to be. If there is one thing that I ask of you, son, it is that you take care of them in my absence." She coughed and covered her mouth. I broke our embrace and took a couple steps away from her. Stopped and frowned.

"Mama, you making it seem like you're giving up. I'm out here every single day fighting for you. Pulling all sorts of schemes and tricks to ensure I am able to come up with at least four thousand dollars, so I can have it to pay for your treatments, and you're basically saying that you're preparing to die? Really?" I felt my temper rising. At the same time, I was getting weaker and weaker, imagining my mother laying in a casket, deceased.

Nobody should have ever had to imagine the sight of that. I started to shake out of fear and anger. She walked over to me and stood in front of me. Reached and placed her hand on my cheek. It felt cold. That made me think about death as well. Then, I started to remember how all of the women looked after Sheek and his men had slain them. It made me sick on the stomach. "Baby, your temper is getting the best of you. The love you have for me is blinding you and shielding you from the present reality. I can fight and fight until the bitter end, but no matter how much I fight, my end is very near. There is nothing we can do about it. I wish there was." She swallowed, and looked down at the ground.

Tears slid down my cheeks, and dropped to the floor. "Yo, I hear what you're saying, but I ain't surrendering to that. I believe you can still beat this thing. Now, I got another two hundred and fifty bands for these doctors. Whatever surgeries or medications you need, Mama, we gon' make sure you get it. I can't lose you. You're all I have. You're my queen, don't forget that? I wouldn't know the first thing about surviving if you weren't here." I was starting to feel sicker imagining her no longer being physically present. I was sure I would lose my mind. She coughed into her fist again. I rubbed her back, and rushed over to grab her juice that was on her table beside her bed. Gave it to her, and ordered her to drink from the straw. She followed my directives. Smacked her lips, and moved away from the juice box.

"They gave me three months, son. If I continue to take the medications, and go through their treatments, we might can squeeze out a few more weeks, but that's it. I'm terminal. But, you know what? I'm okay. I'm ready to go, baby. I'm tired of being sick all of the time. Mama just wants to be whole again. I feel like a prisoner in my own body. This sucks." All I heard was the word, terminal. This made me drop to my knees. I felt so weak, I couldn't think straight. My head was spinning. Even though my mother had been battling the deadly cancer for over two years, it was like the reality of the situation had just kicked in, in that moment. I felt like I was about to become hysterical. I broke down, crying so hard I started to shake, my face turning beet red. My mother had been the only parent I'd ever known.

My father had run away before I was even born. Left my mother to fend for herself in the projects, with no regard for her or the life she was bringing into the world. He was a man I swore I would ever be like. I hated his guts, even though I didn't have a picture of him to put the hate into. Now that my mother was set to leave this earth, I was lost. I didn't know what to do. I felt like killing. I felt like crying. I felt like throwing up. I was wishing I could go in her place. That I could be her sacrifice. I wished she never had to endure any pain, ever, hated that the one weapon that had been formed against her seemed to prosper. She came over and took the time to bend, one knee at a time. Then, she knelt beside me with her arm around my shoulder.

"Baby, I know this news is hard for you to take, but you and I have never kept anything from each other. I didn't want to hold it to myself, and just go out like that. You deserve to know the truth. You are strong, and I know you will get through this. Your fight is for your siblings now. You've done all you can for me, and I love you for it. You're my baby." She kissed my wet cheek, and laid her head against my shoulder. I didn't know what to say, or do. I felt like I should have been the one consoling her.

After all, she was the one set to leave this earth. I felt like I was acting like a wimp and I needed to man up, as hard as it was for me, because I was overly emotional for my mother. I loved her with every fiber of my being. She had been the first person I did, in fact, love and no one had ever come close to the feelings that I had for her. I was at a lost for actions, and words. All I could do was cry, and cry some more. Every time I looked into her beautiful face. I was in disbelief. I became so angry that all I could see was red. I got to my feet and picked her up, carried her to her hospital bed, and laid her down on it. She felt light in my arms. She was only five feet five inches tall, and weighed no more than one hundred pounds even. Before the cancer had taken over, she'd been every bit of one fifty. I hated life so much.

I situated her on the bed, then slid in beside her. Pulled her into my embrace and trapped her in my arms. "Mama, I hear what you're saying, but I ain't ready to let go. I'm gon' fight until the end and you should too. I need you. This world ain't got no purpose for me if you ain't in it." I kissed her lips as more tears dropped out of my eyes, rocked with her back and forth, until she fell asleep in my arms. Sometime during the night, a nurse had come to tell me that visiting hours were over, that I needed to leave the room. I could wait in the waiting room until seven in the morning. But, one murderous glance from me sent her backing out of the room.

"Okay, well as long as you're quiet, I'll let you stay. If anybody asks, just tell them when I did my checks, you were in the bathroom." And with that, she closed the door and didn't come back for the rest of the night. I was glad she hadn't because all I could think about the entire night, was how I was going to get rid of the pain in my heart. The only solution to me was murder. And, it didn't matter whose murder, as crazy as that may have sounded.

* * *

Rayven showed up early the next morning, while there was a blizzard going on outside. She had both Derez and Destiny with her. When the door opened, they rushed in and Destiny made a beeline for the bed, jumping on top of me.

"Kaleb, we ain't seen you in two days. I thought something happened," she said, kissing my cheek, then hugging me as tight as she could. Destiny was twelve years old, and identical to my mother. She had gray eyes and long, thick, wavy hair that flowed down her back. She and Derez were twins. I stood up and held her in the air, planting kisses all over her pretty face. Her cheeks were cold as if she'd just come from outside. She had on a big Chanel leather coat, with a purple scarf around her neck. Her Chanel gloves matched her jacket.

"Sis, I'm good. I been making sure that our mother was protected. Rayven was holding down the fort though, right?"

Derez climbed in the bed and waved Rayven off. "Yeah, right. All these two chickens were doing were running their beaks. They drove me crazy. I couldn't wait to get out there. Word up." He took his skull cap off his head. His waves were deep, and perfect. His eyes, like ours, were gray and bright. He looked a lot like me, but mostly my mother. He hugged her and laid his head on her chest. I felt a twinge of jealousy. I didn't like sharing my mother with nobody. Not even my siblings, as crazy as that may sound.

My mother kissed his cheek. "Boy, hush. You oughta be glad she was there to look after you. Rayven is a God-send." She smiled over at her.

Rayven walked over and kissed my mother's lips. "Thank you, Mama. And, so are you." She came over and took ahold of my hand. "Kaleb, can I holler at you in the hallway for a second? It's important." I glanced over to my mother and she nodded at me.

"Go ahead, baby. See what she want. I'll be okay." Instead of stopping in the hallway, we wound up on the stairwell between flights. Rayven waited until the door closed, before she stepped forward and kissed my lips, wrapping her arms around the back of my neck. I held her waist and tongued her down. She tasted like spearmint. Her perfume was Prada, one of my favorite scents. Even though she had on a big Prada leather jacket, I could feel the heat of her body. Her earmuffs matched the Timbs on her feet. She looked real girly, and sexy as hell to me. I gripped that ass and got into our kiss, until I had her moaning and humping into me. I had visions of hitting that pussy right there on the stairwell. I didn't care if we got caught, especially when she reached in between us and gripped my dick, squeezing it for dear life.

"Umm. Rayven, I'm about to hit this shit real quick, turn around, and put your hands on the wall." I unzipped my Gucci jeans, and pulled my piece out of my boxers.

"What? Boy stop playing. All these doctors and nurses running up and down these stairs. What if we get caught?" she asked. I turned her around and pushed her face first into the wall. Her hands stopped her from bumping her face. She yelped as I yanked her pants down far enough to reveal her purple thong that separated the mounds of her golden ass. They looked chunky. I could smell her perfume from down below, coupled with a hint of her pussy. It made me shake with anticipation. I held her lower back and lined us up.

"What are you doing, Kaleb? You gone get us caught. Uh," she moaned as I slid balls deep into her wet furnace.

As soon as I was buried, I got to long stroking that box and fucking her hard. I knew we didn't have that long, but I needed to release at least one. I had so much on my mind. Needed to be healed. "Un, Rayven, twerk that ass, ma. Hurry up. I need to cum, we can finish this tonight. But, I need to cum right now," I said in a strained voice, watching my dick go in and out of her wet box. The faster I hit it, the louder the scent of her pussy got. She placed a Timb on the first step. Held the wall with both hands and started to twerk hard and fast, swallowing my pole. Her ass jiggled. The pants slid further down her legs and stopped once they were around her ankles. But, she kept on twerking and fucking me like only she could.

"Un. Un. Un. Like that, Kaleb? Like that? Un. Un. Un. Do you like it, daddy? Fuck!" she hollered. The noise echoed in the hallway.

I took ahold of her waist, and started to really pound her out after picking up her rhythm. My piece ran in and out of her, leaking from her juices. I smacked that ass as hard as I could, and felt my nut building inside of me. The sight of that fat ass shaking, and her scents all in the hallway was too much. I slid my thumb into her ass, saw the way it opened to accommodate the digit, and let all of me go into her womb, just as the door opened in the hallway upstairs, and we heard voices. This caused us to scramble to fix our clothes. Cum continued to spill out of my tool, saturating my boxers. We laughed while rushing down the stairs.

T.J. Edwards

Chapter 7

I stayed close to my mother for the next three weeks. Me and Rayven took turns taking care of Derez and Destiny as best we could. I knew it was unfair for me to allow her to take up the burden of them, but I needed to be around my mother as much as possible. I still couldn't fathom the thought of losing her indefinitely. That was my biggest fear, so I took all ninety percent of the money that I had left and paid up her treatments, and for them to perform surgery on her. She needed her right ovary removed because the cancer had spread into it. The surgery would cost ninety thousand alone. The cost didn't matter to me. This was my mother. I dropped the paper with no hesitation. I had to ride for her by any means, and I was.

At the end of the third week, Rayven was finally able to pull me away from my mother's bedside. She said she needed us to have dinner together. That she had some things she wanted to run by me. Things that could potentially help us in the long run monetarily. Long as it was about money I could see no reason why I'd pass up such a meeting. So, I agreed to meet up with her one cold, Thursday night at a barbecue joint out in Queens, called Famous Dave's. Famous Dave's was a nice low-key spot that specialized in some of the best barbecue in the city. I mean, their shit was top notch, and savory. I pulled up at nine at night. It was snowing like crazy, with the wind blowing. It was two weeks away from Thanksgiving, and I was still trying to figure out how I was going to be able to give my siblings a nice meal for that day. I had a few ideas, but I wasn't sure which route I'd take just yet.

Rayven was waiting in the vestibule with a Burberry jacket and scarf on. When she saw me step out of my Monte

Carlo, she broke into the parking lot, and ran into my arms as if she hadn't seen me in weeks. "Baby, I've missed you so freaking much." She hugged me tight, then moved her hair out of her face, before kissing my lips, slow and tenderly. She smelled so good. That was one of the things I loved about her. The scent of a woman was like none other.

"Mmm. I missed you too, boo. How are you doing?" I held her face in my gloved hand, looking into her pretty, captivating brown eyes. She took ahold of my hand and led me toward the restaurant.

"I'm better now. For some reason, I just been yearning for you more and more lately. I feel connected to you and sick when we're apart. Does that sound weird, or too needy to you? Be honest." The wind blew and this made her squint her eyes.

It took my breath away for a second. There were big patches of snow falling from the New York sky. "To be honest with you, Rayven, I been missing you too, boo. I mean, I know we see each other in passing. But, our lives for the last three weeks have consisted of us taking care of either the twins or my mother. I hope you know I appreciate your sacrifices. I owe you, boo. And, you know that as soon as I figure things out, I am going to make sure I repay you. You've been my rider through all of this, fa real." I stopped her, and tongued her ass down, grabbing that juicy ass. Cuffing it so much, she wound up on her tippy toes until I was done, I was hard as hell afterwards. Her body never ceased to have me like that. I think I was obsessed with it or something.

Our kiss broke with a loud pop. Half of her lip gloss had been removed. I could taste it on my tongue. "Kaleb, you already know I have your back. We been riding for each other since elementary. Just because I'm older now and doing my own thing, don't mean I'd ever forget how you stood up for me when we were little, especially when Carl did what he did." Her voice got a little lower. I could tell that she was still embarrassed by the whole thing. I pulled her possessively to me.

"Yo, fuck dude. That punk was a child molester. He got what he deserved. You shouldn't feel no type of way about that either." Carl was a big, black, ugly-ass nigga from the Bronx that Rayven's mother had been married to when we were thirteen years old.

Her mother hadn't been married to him for more than a few months before he started to make nightly visits to Rayven's room. Once there, he'd force himself on her and make her do some unspeakable things. This went on for an entire year, until she told me about it. After I got wind of it, me and Buddy caught him slipping, coming out of Love's liquor store in the Bronx. We waited until he took the alley on his way back to the projects and beat him senseless. To this day, he's still in the wheelchair, paralyzed from the neck down. I wanted to smoke him, but I didn't have a burner back then. She shook her head.

"I don't feel no type of way. I just wish I could get everything out of my brain that he took me through." I held her.

"Yo, it'll happen, ma. You're strong. I got you."

She nodded. "I know you do." She stepped back and looked up at me. "Kaleb, I want you to keep an open mind tonight, okay? I want to introduce you to a few people, and all I'm asking is that you keep an open mind. Can you promise me that?"

"I promise, boo. Let's get inside. It's freezing out here." We stepped into the restaurant and were seated ten minutes later. Rayven handed me a bottle of hand sanitizer. I used a nice amount and checked my surroundings. The place was kind of packed. Dim lights illuminated it just enough to see most of the faces present. After looking them over closely, I didn't detect much of a threat, so I turned my attention back to Rayven. She'd taken off her jacket. Now her perfume really hit me. It smelled so lovely, and arousing. I looked across the table at her and had to admire her beauty.

After all of the years that we'd known each other, she appeared to have gotten finer with time. "So, holler at me, beautiful. What's on your mind?" The waiter came and we placed our orders, giving him back the menus.

"You know how we were talking about finding a way to come up on a bunch of chips?" She looked from right to left as if the other people could hear us. This made me start to look around.

"Yeah, what about it?"

"Well, I've been hollering at a few of the ladies from the club. You know, the ones with children that aren't looking to be dancing for men forever, and I think I've come up with a plan that a put all of us on our feet. I mean, as long as everything goes right." She looked all around again and took a deep breath. I scrunched my face, and scanned the expanse of the establishment. I didn't understand why she was so paranoid, but she was getting me to be that way as well. The one thing I hated was looking over my shoulder. I'd rather dead my enemy than to always be worried about what they were up to.

My nerves were way too bad for that. "Go on."

"Well, you know how the club I work at caters to some of the most prestigious people in the city and abroad, right?"

"Yeah, I'm with you so far. What of it?"

"Baby, most of the men that come in there aren't just looking for dances, they're looking for bed mates, females they can take under their wings, or to make their side pieces. I'm not just talking about your average, every day, run-of-the-mill men either. I'm talking judges, senators, politicians and mob figures, period. Men that run this world, so to speak." She grabbed one of the rolls from the basket of bread in the center of the table. Pinched off it, and placed it into her mouth.

"So, what are you trying to do? You want me to rob them or something?" I asked, confused. I didn't see where she was going with things. I couldn't see myself robbing no judges. If I ever did get caught, that spelled disaster, the same for a politician or mob boss. That was playing with deadly fire, fire that I wasn't willing to get burned by under no circumstances. She sucked her teeth.

"Boy, only bums rob people, I'm talking about some real money. Money that can set us straight for a long period of time each time." She dug in her purse and slapped a bottle of blue pills on the table. "These pills not only fuck you up, but they make you tell your soul. On top of that, the sex is so good to them that it makes them fall in love. Well, for the man anyway. It doesn't do anything for the woman, other than give us a headache and a bunch of gas." She giggled, and slid them across the table to me. I looked them over, opened the top and smelled inside. Jerked my head back and almost threw up. I frowned.

"What the fuck is that smell?" She shrugged her shoulders.

"I don't know, and I don't care. I know they work, and if we use them in the right way, we can have these tricks falling in love and giving us the key to everything they've worked so hard for. I got a few of my girls on deck that I want you to meet tomorrow. These girls will do anything I say, because they trust me not to steer them in the wrong way. I've earned that trust. Now it's time for me, for us, to capitalize off of it. Are you in?" I slid the pills back across the table to her.

"You say you're sure they work? How do you know that for certain?"

She lowered her head, and exhaled. "I had one of my admirers hopped up on one, and he went crazy. Got to talking about how much he love me, and what he wanted to do for me. To make a very long story short, I got fifty grand, and a brand-new Lexus. I don't feel good about it, but at least I know that drug works." I picked the bottle of pills back up and looked them over closely.

"What are they, like some super emotional Viagra or something?" I picked one out of the bottle and held it to my right eye. There was no inscription on it or anything. They looked homemade. Rayven shrugged her shoulders.

"I don't know what they are. One of my Asian friends from the Bronx makes them. She says her mother was doing the same thing back in Korea. It's how they were able to get out of that country. But, that's neither here nor there. These pills are going to make us rich. I mean, the possibilities are limitless." She reached across the table and took ahold of my hand. "Baby, I need to make sure you're with me one hundred percent, before we venture off into this field. It can be dangerous. We're set to cross a lot of powerful people. But, I feel like it's better than you posting up in the projects, like the rest of those low-life dope boys."

I dropped the pill back into the container and twisted the cap, sliding it back across the table to her. "I'm wit it. All we have to do is to come up with a nice strategy on how we're about to strip these dudes. Get in fast, get as much money as we can, then stop. That's what we have to do. When do I meet the other girls?"

"A week. My girl, Sven, will have us about ten bottles then. I will have my girls ready. We'll get at their richest tricks and go from there." She batted her eyelashes. "But, that has nothing to do with tonight. Tonight is for me." I was confused.

"What do you mean?" She took my hand and kissed the back of it.

"I just want you to spend some time worshipping my body. Take that big ol' thang between your legs and do me right. You know, make the baby feel all good and whatnot." I smiled and looked around the restaurant. Everybody seemed to be engaged in their own things. The waiters hung to one side of the restaurant, talking amongst themselves in between the times they traveled back and forth with food, or drinks for the patrons.

I slid around to the side of the table that Rayven was sitting on. Since we were in a booth, this made it a lot easier for what I had in mind. I placed my arm around her shoulders. I kissed her hot neck, and trailed my tongue up and down. "I'm saying, you know how I get down, baby. I can start appreciating this body right now. You know how crazy I am about you." I sucked her neck, and ran my nose up and down. Her scent was doing something to me, as usual. She reached under the table into my lap and unbuckled my belt, before sliding her hand into my pants, taking ahold of my pipe, squeezing it.

"I want you to get on your knees right now, and eat my kitten. I don't care who see, or if we get caught. I want your tongue inside me now, daddy." She pulled my piece above my waistband, and started to stroke it up and down, running her thumb in circles around the head. It sent chills through me. I shivered and my dick got harder, standing straight up.

I looked both ways again, then I got on my knees between her legs. She shimmied her jeans down to her ankles. I ducked under her calf muscles, stuck my face right in her crease and took a big whiff of her perfume-scented pussy. "Damn, ma." Yanked her thong to the side and opened her lips wide, slurped her juices. Then, my tongue was going up and down her slit at full speed. She tasted slightly salty, and sweet. I sucked her clit into my lips. Trapped it and ran my tongue in quick circles around it. Nipped it with my teeth, just enough to make her jerk in her seat. She opened her legs wider and slid her fingers into her gap, trying to insert them into her hole. I licked all over them, before moving them out of the way. I didn't need any help. I knew how to make her cum, had been doing it ever since we were twelve years old. When I removed her fingers, she groaned and started to shake. I licked all over her exposed thighs. Biting into them, then trailed my tongue back to her gap, sucked two fingers into my mouth, sliding them into her tight hole, running them in and out of her.

She gripped the sides of the table and got to riding them fast. "Un. Un. Daddy, daddy, daddy. You gon' make me cum," she whispered. "You're playing wit me so good." I drove them into her faster and faster. My tongue attacked her clit as if it were mad at it. Her juices ran out of her and onto the booth. She scooted to the edge of the seat, and opened her thighs as far as they could go. I pinched her clit and slid my tongue into the crack of her ass, twirling it around her anus. Her taste had my piece so hard that it was throbbing well past my navel. My fingers were a blur going in and out of her. Her juices dripped off of my chin. Her toes scrunched together. "I'm cumming, daddy. I'm cumming. Oh my fucking God!" She humped into my face at full speed, grabbed me by the back of the head and forced me into her box even more. Now, her juices were running down my neck, and into my shirt. Her scent was heavy. She shook and came for the second time and pushed me away, breathing hard just as our waiter came to the table, his presence making me bump my head loudly.

* * *

As soon as Rayven slid her key into the lock, and the door swung inward, I picked her lil ass up, and rushed inside with her. She sucked all over my lips, moaning into my mouth, while I held my tongue out for her to taste. I crashed with her into the wall. She got down, and I pulled her pants down and off of her body. She kicked them away, and stepped back up to me, fumbling with my belt and jeans. "I want you, daddy. I want you so bad that my kitty is aching like never before." Her lips met mine again as my pants fell to my ankles. My dick was sticking straight up, feening for her sexy body. I gripped that big booty, slid my hand into her crease from the back, playing with her pussy lips. Finally, my two middle fingers slid inside her warmth, sliding in and out at full speed, before I slid them upward, and fingered her asshole. I wanted some of that too.

She shook her head and fell to her knees. Grabbed my boxers, slid them down and off. Took my dick and stroked it, before sucking it into her mouth. Her head went crazy in my lap. The sounds were loud and nasty. Enough to push me to the edge before she even got started all the way. I groaned, and pushed her head back. "Nall, boo, you said tonight all about you, right?" I picked her up, and set her on her kitchen table. She laid on her side and lifted her leg all the way up in the air, while my tongue ran up and down her ass crack. I held her waist, and slid it in and out of her back door, playin' wit her clitoris along the way.

"Un. Un. Daddy. I. Daddy. I want you to fuck me right now. I can't take it no more!" she hollered. Beat her fist on the table and came when I pinched her clit and started to finger her ass fast and hard.

I stood up, and pulled her to the edge. Stroked my dick five quick times, and brought it to her slit. Grabbed her hips and slammed it home. "Fuck, daddy!" She wrapped her arms around my neck and bit my chest hard. Her breathing was labored. "Hit this pussy, daddy. Hit it hard just like you always do! Please!" I cocked back and slammed home hard, then did it again, and again. Her pussy was so wet that it began to ooze out of her and onto the table. The legs threatened to give out, but I didn't care. I would let her fall. For as long as she had been a part of my life I never had. This was my baby. My right-hand against all odds. I pulled her closer to me, and dug my fingers into her flesh, hitting it harder and harder. I was trying to reach her heart from inside her pussy.

"Damn, ma. Baby. This pussy. Shit. This heat, ma. This heat got me." I closed my eyes and kept going.

She pulled her top off, and exposed her breasts. Both nipples stood at attention. She pulled them from their mounds. I watched them pop back and stand tall. Sweat glistened on her forehead. She had her mouth wide open with her head thrown back. Her long hair fell over her shoulders. "Daddy. Daddy. Cum in me, daddy. I'll do anything for you, daddy. Anything." She leaned forward and dug her nails into my back, wrapping her thick thighs around my waist. Fucking me back like a savage of a queen. I picked her up and fell to the kitchen floor with her. My ass rising and falling. Plunging and plunging, trying to hit her deepest regions. Her walls sucking at me and spitting her cream all over my pole. It felt glorious. I couldn't get enough of it. I was becoming addicted all over again.

"Ma, I'm bout to cum in this pussy. I'm bout to cum in this wet ass pussy! Aw shit, boo! I can't help it." I forced her into a ball, diving deep. My whole body locked up, and then I was cumming in rivers. Deep in her womb. She dug her nails in me. Threw her head back and screamed in my ear before cumming again.

T.J. Edwards

Chapter 8

I met the girls eight days later, at the Hyatt Regency Hotel in upper Manhattan. It was Friday afternoon, and each of the women were set to go to work that night at the club. I was a little nervous at first, because I didn't know how they were going to take to me. Rayven had told me up front that all four of them were bad bitches. Chicks she considered to be on her level, and I knew from experience that she thought highly of herself, physically, as she should have. I was a street nigga, and my chips were a little funny. Most of the women in New York wouldn't give you the time of day if your chips weren't sitting right. These were strippers that were used to being around the upper echelon of New York, whereas I was from the Harlem projects. I had not even been outside of New York since I was a little kid, and my mother took me to Haiti for a funeral. So, I was kind of nervous. Because my money was so funny, I felt less than. Like a bum. A nobody. A degenerate. I could barely look myself in the eye when I looked into the mirror.

Rayven had rented the room, and I felt like a bum because I couldn't even help her with the fee. She assured me I was good and I was overthinking things, but she couldn't convince my brain of that. She walked out of the small kitchen, and into the living room with a bottle of Ace of Spades. "Daddy, chill. Like I told you before, I got these women. They follow behind me, and since I look up to you, they will too. Just be yourself, and put your foot down. The goal is to get rich. That's it, that's all." She handed me the bottle, and then a cigar stuffed with Harlem Red, which was some of the best weed in the city. It had been imported from Maui, but since the Bloods had the connect on it, they called it Harlem Red, so I did too. Rayven put out a silver platter, and poured about a half-ounce of cocaine on it. Placed a divider in the middle of it, and poured about seven grams of China White on that side. Then, she put a red sticker on the side the heroin was on and a yellow sticker for the cocaine. She looked over at me and smiled.

"Chill out, daddy. I gotta make sure I feed each one of these bitches' habits. There ain't a stripper in the game that don't have one." There was a knock at the door as she finished this sentence. She dusted her Prada skirt dress off, and threw her hair over her shoulders.

"And what's your habit?" I asked, curious by her statement. She smiled.

"My habit is your crazy ass, and maybe a Percocet from time to time." She stepped to the door and opened it. "Hey girl, 'bout time you made it." I saw her step into the hallway, and a pair of white arms encased her body. The next thing I knew, she was holding the hand of a bad-ass white girl. I say bad because this lil chick was fine as hell to me, and I have never been the one to jock white chicks like that. "Baby, this is Rabbit. Rabbit, this my daddy right here, and our first line of defense."

Rabbit stepped all the way into the hotel room. She was five feet two inches tall. Thick. She had big titties and a slim waist, with a nice ass on her. She took off her Fendi leather, faced me with both of her nipples poking through her blouse. Her stomach was flat. Her eyes were green, and electric. She had big lips, and a pretty face. Her nails were done with Fendi symbols all over them. She was well put together. She walked over to me and opened her arms. Hugging my frame. "Since you're her daddy, you might as well be mines too. Rayven say you all about your bread, so if that's what's good, then I'ma fuck wit you the long way. I got a team of white hoes that need guidance, but first things first." She grabbed the bottle of Ace out of my hands and turned it up. Then, she leaned over the table of goodies, picking up a pinkie nail full of heroin, and tooting it.

The next stripper to walk through the door was Trix. Trix was Puerto Rican and black. Bad. Strapped, with a little frame. She had to be about five feet even. Brown eyes, big lips, and an ass so big it had to be fake. I didn't know if it was or not, but it went nice with her shape. Her thighs were kind of slim, which is what made me think that the ass was a little off base, but whatever. She came into the room, kissed Rayven on the lips and went right for the heroin as well. She spoke in a strong Spanish accent, that Rayven and Rabbit didn't have no problem understanding, but I did. It took me a minute. The last stripper showed up ten minutes after Trix. Her name was Ghana. She was dark-skinned with some of the smoothest skin I had ever seen on a woman. She was five feet seven inches tall. Beautiful. Dark brown eyes and big lips. She was slightly bow legged, and had a body to die for. Out of all the ones that had shown up, she was the baddest to me. She had wavy hair that was shaved on both sides. Her diamond game was on point, as well as her nails. Her make-up was minimal.

She walked up to me and slid her arms around my neck. "Damn, you're way finer than what Rayven let on. Mmm. I like that." She kissed my cheek, then sucked on my ear lobe. Took a step back, and looked me up and down. "But, I'm letting you know right now that good looks don't pay the bills. For me, it's all about the money. Never get that twisted. You feel me. I represent more than just me." She ran her tongue across her upper row of teeth, and stepped to the table, and scooped up a nice portion of the cocaine, before sitting on the love seat off by herself. Sven showed up with her laptop in hand. She was a short and skinny Asian chick, with light eyes, and long jet black hair that was highlighted with gray. She took a seat on the couch and opened her laptop, typing away on the keys.

"Alright, now I apologize for being late, but that weather screwed me over. There are crashes everywhere." She continued to type while the other girls did their drugs of choice. Rayven sipped from the bottle of Ace, and handed it back to me.

"Girls, there are three things that I will always need from each of your tricks in order to tap into their finances and lives. I'll need their social security numbers, at least one major credit card number and the pass code, and lastly their home address. Not one where they may be more apt to take you, I'm talking the ones they share with their families. That is very important." She typed some more, before setting the laptop on top of the table and turning it around, so that it faced Rayven. "Rayven, your man is worth fifteen million dollars altogether. He has five million in the bank. Five million in property, and five million linked into investments on wall street. He grosses five hundred thousand dollars a year, and is set for a raise in three months. His raise put him as a junior partner. He'll make seven hundred and fifty thousand a year after that. He's the kind of trick that we're targeting, ladies.

"Keep in mind that we are not chasing after lookalike rich men. Those fools that parade around with a bunch of jewelry, and talk the game, are doing just that, talking the game. Real rich men rarely ever boast in words. They allow for their actions to do the talking. I'll only give you three strikes to bring me fake tricks. Upon the third time, I'm done with you all around the board. Another thing, my cut is twenty-five percent on all transactions. Even in blackmail. That will include my pills, time and energy invested.

Everybody got that?" She looked around, awaiting confirmation from everyone in the room.

"I can't believe Justin is worth fifteen million dollars. I didn't believe him when he said he'd make my dreams come true. I don't even know what to say·." She scrolled down the screen and covered her mouth.

Rabbit stood up, and handed Sven a piece of paper. "Huh, that's everything you said I needed. I even got some extra credit shit on there, just to help you out. I wanna know what he working with. I'm a night away from laying down with him and before I do, I wanna make sure it's going to be worth my while." She placed a tuft of blonde hair behind her ear lobe. Sven took the piece of paper and entered the information into the computer. He did a series of typing, then turned the computer around so Rabbit could see it.

"Girl, he's broke. He's worth two hundred thousand, and in the middle of a messy divorce. All of his assets are tied up until further notice. Don't even waste your time." Rabbit looked the screen over, and scrunched her face. "I should have known something wasn't up. Damn, and he cute too." I was taken aback because I thought that two hundred plus thousand was a decent amount of money. I was sitting on less than five grand, so if they was looking down on dude like that, I wondered how they'd look down on me when they found out my net worth.

"Okay, Sven. Once you're able to see all of this information, then what? How do we get the money out of them without them knowing?" Rayven asked, sliding next to me, and laying her head on my shoulder. Sven smiled.

"It's very simple. I'll take a little at a time. Take a percentage of their investments, and returns. Pinch off money from their salaries. Any transactions that they make I'll be able to see them. Being that I work for Secure Lock, no transaction will miss me. And then when that gets a little hot, that is when we will move into blackmail, so you ladies have to be sure you take lots of pictures. The pictures taken will be used against them at a later date. This is why it is crucial for you to seek powerful married men. Men that have political or prestigious careers where public opinion is very important. A rich man's reputation is everything, especially in the cutthroat social climate of New York City."

I nodded my head. I liked how this lil Asian chick thought. "Yo, so what am I here for then?" I needed to know, because it sounded like Sven had everything down to a science. I didn't see what place I had in any of this, and I was starting to feel some type of way to say the least. Rayven stood up, and cleared her throat.

"He's probably the only man we can trust in this city. Once we hit the ground running, we're going to need protection. Kaleb represents a mob of lunatics that answer to him and only him. One word from him and they'll murder in droves. Trust me on this. On top of that, he is a man of integrity. His agenda is pure. I've told all of you about his mother, my mother, and what we're trying to accomplish. Each and every last one of you has had somebody in the family that has passed away from cancer. We're all connected in some way. We need each other, not just for this cause, but because we desire a better life. Ghana, you have your whole family back in Africa that is leaning on you. Trix, yours is back in Puerto Rico.

"Rabbit, you're trying to get your sisters out of foster care. Sven, you feed your entire village back in North Korea. We have to bind together and make this happen, and in order to do that, we're going to need guidance and security. Kaleb will see to it that we're good." All of the girls looked at each other, and nodded their heads, then dropped them as if

Rayven had said something that left them in deep thought. Sven winced and closed her eyes as if she were in pain.

"I don't know you, Kaleb, but I trust Rayven. She's a good judge of character and all she talks about is you. So I'll trust her enough to trust you." She stood up and extended her hand. We shook. "There is guaranteed to be some form of drama ahead. Make sure you're always ready for the unknown. Our lives will depend on that, sooner or later." I nodded, and pulled her in for a hug. I didn't like the scent of her perfume. She also cringed within our embrace. That rubbed me the wrong way.

I waited until she sat down before I said anything. "Look, I don't know you girls like that, but I'm willing to gain your trust, and ride for you like no other man in this city. I'm starving. I see how you looked down on a man with two hundred something thousand in the bank, and I'm like damn, I ain't even got five bands put up. I got a mother in the hospital fighting for her life. Two siblings that depend on me, and when I can't step up to the plate as a man, then Rayven does. I'm ready for change. I gotta get my shit together and provide for my people. I swear, if y'all a give me a chance, I'll hold you down. That's my word, and my word is everything to me." I looked from one female unto the next. They were either looking at the floor, or directly at me. "All I need is a shot."

Rabbit smiled. "I swear to God, that nigga is fine. I'm trying my best to listen to his spiel and shit, but I can't help imagining his ass naked. I can see his print in his jeans and everything." She giggled.

Trix laughed. "I was just about to say that. You took the words right out of my mouth." She looked up at me. "Yo, Kaleb chill, lil daddy. I'm in. Just keep shit one hunnit wit me and this Puerto Rican bitch is all in. I got some nice tricks lined up with cash. All I need for you to do is to guide me, and to make sure I'm safe. You do that, and I'll times that five gees you stressing about by fifty in a few moves. I'm sure of that."

"Yeah, I'm in too," Rabbit said, standing up and sliding her arm around my lower back. She glanced at Rayven. "Say, ma, we gon' be able to climb aboard his fine ass though right?" She looked into my gray eyes. "I'm saying, kid got all of my juices flowing. I'm ready to bring his ass a bag right now. You fuck wit white hoez, Kaleb?" She licked her juicy lips.

Rayven stood up. "Bitch, dick ain't free, and it ain't about to be just about sex. If we're all getting in the bed together, it's because we're on some family shit. If that's what it is, then yeah, my nigga can lay that pipe. Ain't that right, daddy?" I was at a loss for words, but I had to roll with the punches. I was trying to not focus on the fact that every female in that room was super bad. Some of the baddest females I had ever seen in my life. They could probably have any man they wanted. Any man could have stood in my place, but here I was.

"It's all love, long as we're all family." I placed my arm around Rabbit's back. Rayven slid under my other one. Trix got up and kissed my cheek. "It's a family affair then, papi." All that was left was Ghana. She sat on the couch, drinking from the bottle of Ace. She slammed the bottle down, and wiped her mouth. Her eyes were bloodshot.

"My whole life, men have done nothing but fucked me over. Even back home in my village, they can't be trusted." She snorted and spit a loogey on the carpet beside her and stood up, walked over to us. She reached into her Gucci bag, and came out of it with a spear that looked as if it were made out of stone. She dropped the bag, and lowered her eyes. The girls scattered. "Ten men I've killed with this right here. Ten souls. Don't be the eleventh one. I trust no man. You cross me, and I'll eat your penis while you're still alive." She said this with her eyes bucked. Stared at me for a long time, sending goose bumps all over me, then smiled. "I'm in. Let's make it happen." She sat back on the couch and crossed her thick thighs.

She was a crazy one, I could tell. I would have to play her close, and make sure I never slipped up with her. After we all got an understanding, everything was set in motion. The girls went off in pursuit of rich tricks, and I sat back and waited until my number was called. Rayven went into Puppet Master mode and made sure that she had a hand in everything each woman did. Because she had her hand inside of all of their pots, mine was inserted as well. In a matter of two months, I was sitting on thirty thousand. I couldn't complain. We were just getting started.

T.J. Edwards

Chapter 9

After three months of intense grinding with the girls, I'd reached sixty thousand dollars, and was able to cop myself a 2020 Benz G-Wagon. It was black on black, with the gold Parelli's. The interior was all red leather, and I got it hooked up with everything Sony, even the four, nine-inch televisions inside of it. It was just a start for my comfort, but it put a smile on my face. I made sure that Derez and Destiny had top-notch school clothes, boots and shoes for the winter months, and all of the bills were paid up through 2019. I felt like I was making leeway. My family was secure, and for me that is what it was all about. Buddy hit me up going into the fourth month of me, and the girl's hustling and said it was imperative that I met up with him as soon as possible. That he had some shit to run by me.

Life or death type shit. I didn't know what he was talking about, but the first thing that came to my mind was Sheek. I hadn't really kicked it in Harlem ever since we took Sheek and his men out. I just got an eerie feeling every time I rolled through that borough, so I tried to avoid it. I didn't want to meet up with the homie there either, but I felt like I'd been snubbing him ever since the hit. So, I met up with him, one Wednesday afternoon, in front of the Harlem River Projects. He came out of the building and popped the collar on his bomber jacket. It was freezing out, and it was early February. I didn't know when the harsh winter was going to let up, but I couldn't wait. When he saw me step out of my wagon, he smiled, and made his way toward me. I was Gucci down from the skull cap, to my scarf, all the way down to the boots on my feet. My dreads were freshly twisted, hanging lovely. I felt good. I had a few chips in the bank. My mother was still fighting, and alive.

I felt like I was on the verge of something great. I slammed the door, and made my way over to him. We embraced in front of the Projects. "Yo, what's good, money? Long time no see," I said, palming the back of his head as I hugged him. He smelled funny to me, like funk and alcohol.

"Yo, where you been at, Dunn? I got all kinds of heat on my head. Word up." He stepped back, looking me over. "You ain't fucking wit me or somethin?" He looked hurt, and angry. I shook my head.

"I been on my grind, son. You know I gotta make it happen for my people. That's all. I been trying to stay away from Harlem. Ain't nothin' but trouble out here. What's the word?"

"We gotta sit down in front of that nigga, Gorilla, kid. Son sent for us, you already know what that mean." He lowered his head and shook it. "Yo, I don't know what to do." Gorilla was one of the old heads that called shots over all of the hustlers in Harlem. He was the first gangster to make two million in a week, back in the eighties.

Since then, he'd managed to rise above the slums. He was fucking around with real estate, and had owned twenty percent of the New York Knicks. Even though his residence was no longer in Harlem, he felt like it was still his borough and he carried on like it was. I knew for a fact that Sheek was taking orders from him. This worried me. I didn't want to go to war with a nigga like Gorilla. Not while everything was flowing so smoothly with the girls. "Nall, fuck Blood. I ain't fucking wit that nigga, kid. He ain't got no good news. If that fool calling for a meeting, that mean he ready to dead us. He must caught wind about what happened to Sheek. Think we got something to do with it."

"So, what we gon' do, man?" Buddy asked, looking worried.

"I ain't gon' do shit. I'm about to bounce. Fuck Harlem. I ain't got time for these streets no more. I want out of this shit, B. Word up." I turned my back on Buddy and began to walk to my wagon. He grabbed my arm and turned me around.

"So, you just gon' leave me behind, nigga? Really?" He frowned his face as the wind blew.

I yanked my hand away. "Get the fuck off of me. You ain't gotta stay here. You know that fool, Gorilla, on bullshit. Why would you have a sit-down with that fool, huh?" I was getting heated. Sometimes that nigga Buddy acted so stupid to me, like he didn't get the most obvious of things.

"How the fuck I'ma leave, son? I ain't got no scratch to do that. Everybody can't come up like you did. Riding Benz wagons and all that shit. Gucci all over ya ass and stuff. I'm hurting. So, either put me on, or come to this meeting with the god. Which is it going to be?" He looked me up and down. The smoke coming out of his mouth was horrible. I think he might have missed a few days of brushing his teeth. Maybe the stress of Gorilla was getting the better of him.

"Nigga, you had three hundred and seventy five thousand dollars, just like I did. What happened to it?" He smacked his lips, and waved me off.

"That was months ago, Blood. Bills and all type of shit ate that money away. Are you gon' put me on or not?" He wiped his mouth, and rubbed it on his pants legs. "We supposed to be family."

"How much bread you talking, kid?" I reached into my pocket and pulled out two gees, ready to give it to him.

"In order to get away from son, I'm thinking at least fifty stacks. That should get me right. Either that or a few kilos of that boy. Nah' mean? The cost of living is higher than the

Statue of Liberty's knees." He pulled out a Newport and lit it, after shielding the lighter in his hand to get it lit.

"Buddy, on everything, I almost just punched you in your shit, nigga. How the fuck is you gon' ask me for fifty gees, like I'm holding like that? Let's be real, nigga. I was thinking a few gees, not no fucking fifty," I spat, getting vexed.

"Blood, two gees won't even keep me high for the rest of the week." He started to scratch the back of his neck, and then his arms. His lips were dry and white. It was then that something hit me. I had to ask him to make sure of it, though.

"Bruh, are you fucking with that shit? Huh?" The big project buildings seem to sway behind him. People came in and out of the doors, bracing themselves for the cold. He smiled, and shrugged his shoulders.

"My wrist been fucking wit me. Bree left, and took our daughter with her. I'm tired of being in pain. This shirt hurts. So, yeah, I been fucking with that raw. It's been getting by. But, what nigga in Harlem ain't?" He continued to scratch himself, now more vigorously.

"What? That boy? Nigga, hell nall. I ain't got shit for you 'cause you ain't gon' do shit but shoot it up. I can't believe you." I waved him off and made my way back to my truck.

"You can't turn your back on me, Kaleb. You can't leave me in Harlem, son. It's your fault that my hand is gone. Your fault that Bree left. I'm fucked up, man." he fell to his knees. I turned around just as they were landing in the snow.

"What did you say about your hand?" I turned around and started walking back toward him.

"I know you took the money for your mother. I knew the same night they cut my hand off, but I understood. I understood and I didn't say shit. How could I? You're my

94

muthafuckin' brother." He broke out in tears. "Yo, I ain't got shit no more. Bree gone. Don't nobody give a fuck about me. You the one person I thought did, but now you leaving me too. Of course, I'm using." He knelt all the way forward, and placed his face in the snow. I could hear his sobs. People came and walked around him as if he were some sort of plague. I rushed to his side, and picked him up.

"Yo chill, son. It's gon' be all right. I didn't know all of that was on your mental. I didn't know they were going to cut off your hand either. I owe you for that burden, bruh. Yo, I owe you big time."

He shook his head. "I need Bree back, Kaleb. I need my baby back. I can't function without her. And, what we gon' do about Gorilla? He said that if we don't come to him, he gon' come to us. And that if he have to do that, expect the worst."

"Yo, fuck Gorilla, kid! Fuck that nigga, B.! I ain't stressing over him right now. I'ma get Bree back for you and help y'all get the fuck out of Harlem. That's on my plate right now. Aight?" He nodded in my chest. Up close, his breath was killing me. I tried to hold mine, but I could only do it for so long.

"Yo, just get Bree back for me, and we'll go from there. Gorilla ain't gon' be back in town until Saturday. Hopefully, we're out of Harlem by then." He broke our embrace and wiped his face. "I'm sick, kid. I need a few ends." I gave him five hundred dollars, and put him up in the Capitol Inn Suites right outside of Harlem by the expressway.

* * *

I rang the doorbell, and dusted my pants off. Blew my breath into my hand and smell the air around it, before popping a stick of Extra gum into my mouth. The spearmint spread all around real quick, and I liked that. Bree answered the door, and popped back on her legs. Looked off and rolled her eyes. "Kaleb, let me guess, that bum-ass nigga sent you over here to do his bidding for him." She smacked her lips and looked up at me. I handed her a roll of hundreds, totaling five gees even.

"Huh, this for you. Buddy told me to give this to you when I got here." She took the money and thumbed through it.

"Boy, yeah right. That nigga ain't never gave me no paper like this. Besides, ya mans is a heroin addict now. He's out there. Ain't no way that fool a be sending me no five gees. Come in." I stepped through the threshold and she stepped on her tippy toes and wrapped her arms around my neck. Kissing my cheek, and then my lips. It wasn't the first time that we'd kissed on the lips since her and Buddy had been together.

We'd even done it a few times in front of Buddy, it was no big deal. But, this time, her kiss lasted a little longer than before. And I felt her trying to slip her tongue past my lips. I had to pat her ass and push her back just a bit. "Hold fast, ma, what you on?" I wiped my mouth, still tasting her lip gloss on my tongue. She laughed, stepped past me and locked the door to the small apartment. It felt incredibly hot, like she had the heat all the way up or something. She had on a pair of red lace boy shorts. And a black tank top that showed off her stomach. She stepped back into the living room with a smirk on her face and waved the roll of hundreds in front of me.

"Nigga, ever since I been messin' wit him, you've always been the one footing the bill for everything. You don't think I know that?" she asked, directing me to have a seat. I sat, and spaced my legs. Took my phone out of my pocket, and sat it on the table.

"Yo, I'm supposed to step in when my mans ain't handling his bidness. You forget that I knew you before I did him. Plus y'all got a daughter. I can't allow for the homie to be slipping up like that." Bree sat the money on the table, and pushed it across it.

"I don't want you cleaning up his messes no more, Kaleb. Sooner or later, he has to be a man. As long as you're being the man for him, he'll never learn how to be one himself." She sat back and crossed those thick thighs. I could see a hint of cellulite. That just meant that her body was au natural. I picked up the money and slammed it on the table.

"Like I said before, there is a child involved. Breeyonna is my god-daughter. Long as I'm breathing, I'ma make sure you're straight, so you can make sure she's straight. Now, take this money before I buss ya ass." I warned. She took it, and squeezed the bills in her little fist.

"When did he start shooting that dope, Kaleb? You ain't fucking with that shit now, are you?" She looked over at me, both concerned and angry. I shook my head.

"Nall, I ain't battling that demon just yet, but only God knows where the slums of Harlem is going to lead me. Son, been through a lot. I think he just broke before I did. I don't want to hold that against him. Nobody is the same."

She shook her head. "I ain't fucking wit that nigga no more, Kaleb. He ain't nothin' but a pull me down. He ain't got nothin' going for himself. He ain't an asset to me, or Breeyonna. Tell him to move on with his life. I ain't gon' even waste my time putting him on child support, because it's only a matter of time before he down on a hundred and twenty fifth, with the rest of the needle heads trying to sell hot merchandise. I just want him to leave us alone. Can I get you something to drink?" She stood up and headed for the kitchen. Her panties were deep in her ass crack, leaving the bottom halves of her cheeks exposed. I couldn't help peeping them. She caught me looking at them, and smirked up once again. "I don't know why you be acting like you ain't curious as to how I get down in that bedroom. I'm woman enough to say that I been feeling you for years now. I still think you're the finest man I've ever seen in person. Hand to God. Now the drink. What do you want?"

"Any type of juice is cool. My mouth a lil dry." I wiped the sweaty palms of my hands on my pants and exhaled loudly. I was bogus for peeping Bree like that. Given she was strapped and looked good as hell to me, but this was my mans' baby mother. I was supposed to be over here patching things up for him, not lusting off of her body and shit. Man, it was so hard not to though. Bree was all project, and super jazzy. That sexy kind. She came back into the living room and handed me a glass of fruit punch, with three ice cubes inside of it.

"Here you go." I took it.

"Thank you. Where is Breeyonna?" I asked, looking around the small living room. There was barely any furniture inside of it. A three-piece living room set, and a wooden table in the middle. A fifty-inch television hung on the wall, to the left of it was an entertainment system.

"She's with her grandmother. Why, did he tell you to ask me that too, or are you just concerned for yourself?" She smiled, and took a sip of her juice. Got up, and started messing with the entertainment system, until Jhené Aiko's "New Balance" was crooning out of the speakers. The music was soothing. Bree's panties were so far in her ass now that both cheeks were out. She looked over her shoulder at me.

"Bree. You know your cheeks are hanging out for me to see. What are you on, ma?" I sat the glass on the table. She walked over to me and stood in between my legs.

"Kaleb, I been feeling you ever since we were kids. I ain't fucking wit Buddy no more, no matter what he have you do. Son is a scrub, and I got goals he ain't trying to help me reach. What's good with you? I saw you pull up in a Benz G-Wagon, them joints ain't cheap. How can I be down?" She slowly straddled my lap and took my head into her hands. Placed her forehead against mine and kissed my lips with her eyes closed.

I gripped that ass, and rubbed all over it, slid my hand downward all in the crotch of her panties. I could feel the heat beating against the material. Her lips were prominent. I pressed on them, searching for the hole. My dick was super hard in my jeans. "Un, damn, Kaleb. Let's just do it this one time. He ain't gotta know shit. I swear, if you just get me right, I'll play my role with him, but my heart ain't there no more. it just ain't." She reached behind herself and yanked her panties all the way to the side, exposing her pussy lips, then brought my fingers to them. "Feel that? You see how wet you got me?" My fingers played up and down her wet slit, while she sucked on my neck, moaning. I opened her hole further, and my middle finger went inside of her. She felt tight and there was a lot of resistance. Even if I wanted to, I knew I couldn't fit inside of her.

"Damn Bree, why this pussy so tight like this?" I was breathing hard, trying to find my will power. I knew I was bogus. She started to undo my pants. Scooted backward and fell to her knees.

"I ain't fucked that nigga, in eight months, and I ain't been doing shit. I been turned off. I'm one of those females that I can only do something if my emotions are in check, and they haven't been. But, now I'm feening. You gotta give me some of this, Kaleb. I swear, I won't say nothin'. That's on my daughter." She pulled my pants back enough so that my dick sprung up. Her eyes got big. "Damn boy, I thought Rayven was lying." She squeezed it, and sniffed the head, then licked all around the helmet, before her mouth was going up and down it like a professional. She'd pump it with her hand, then swallow me again. I sat back on the couch, and I couldn't get Buddy's face out of my head. But, it felt so damn good. I pushed Bree back.

"Yo chill, I can't do this, ma. That's my nigga. I'm feeling ya head game and all that, but that's my dude. What I look like cumming all down ya throat?"

She groaned and sucked the helmet as hard as she could. "As much as he cheat on me? Besides, we ain't married. We don't owe each other nothing. I'm feening, Kaleb." She pumped my dick up and down real fast and sniffed my balls. "This a lot of meat. It's what I been missing." She stood up and pulled her panties off, then rubbed in between her bald lips. My dick was jumping like crazy. I had never been so hot in my life. She looked so good with her thick thighs, and the dark gap in between them. She played with it just enough to flash some of her pink. That sent a bolt of horniness through me.

"Fuck! Yo shorty, come here, man. Damn!" I reached for her and pulled her to me. She straddled my waist and leaned forward. I lined us up. Set the head right at her opening, and slowly eased her down, until she swallowed the whole pipe, digging her nails into my shoulders. She took quick breaths and sat still with me planted deep in her belly.

"Okay. Okay. Kaleb. Now please baby, just let me do me." She kissed my lips, rose and slammed down hard on me. Then did it again, and again. Before I knew it, she was

100

bouncing up and down like crazy. I held my legs straight out under me, clenching my teeth together. Her pussy was hot and wet. I was shivering it was so good. "Kaleb. Kaleb. You're finally in me. You're finally inside of me. Uh! Yes. Yes. Yes, Yes. Yes. I'm riding this dick. This big ass dick. Uh. Riding it. Ooo. Fuck." She bounced higher and higher. Threw her head back, moaning louder and louder. I rubbed all over her juicy ass. Sniffed at the air to get a whiff of her secret scent. It took a little while, and slowly but surely it rose into the air, and this completed my jubilee. She grabbed the back of the couch and got to fucking me as hard as she could. "Yo fine ass. Yo fine ass. I needed. I needed this dick. Uh! Uh! Kaleb! Yes!

She popped her ass over and over. Hugged me and came, shaking against my body. Her hot breath blowin' into my face. It smelled like fruit punch and Doublemint gum. I flipped her over and got behind her. Grabbed her hair, and slid back into her body, fucking her hard from the back, while she huffed and puffed with her mouth wide open. "Kaleb, Aw yes. Hit this shit! Kill it, Kaleb. Look at my ass. Oh, like before. Look at my ass like you were before. See it jiggle. Shit! Shit! Shit!" she screamed. I was stabbing it with precision. Raised my hand and slammed it into her fleshy ass. Beating them walls in. It felt so good. Wasn't nothing like fucking a thick woman. Nothing. She bounced back into me faster and faster, while I attacked that ass with my open palm. Slapping and diving deeper and deeper, until it became too much for me. I pulled out, stroked my dick up and down and came in spurts all over her rounded ass in thick droplets. Her face was wedged into the corner of the couch. She screamed and came again.

* * *

I gave her another two bands and opened the door to her apartment. I'd stopped and caught a quick shower. The whole time the water sprayed into my face, my conscience got the best of me. I couldn't believe I'd slipped the way I did. I should have been a better man. I was hating myself on the way out the door. "Wait, Kaleb. What is this money for? Huh? Is because you're feeling guilty about what we just did?" she asked, pulling her robe around her naked body. She'd grabbed a quick shower after I'd gotten out. She held the money at face level. Two females came out of the apartment directly across from hers. They looked me up and down and laughed to themselves. They appeared to be Puerto Ricans as was most of the building. I waited until they walked off, before I responded to her.

"Nah, ma, it ain't just because of that. I just wanna make sure you're good. I mean, I can't lie. I am feeling some type of way, but I'll get over it. I think what we did was long overdue. It is what it is." I was about to close the door when she grabbed me by my jacket.

"Kaleb, wait, this money is only going to hold me for so long. I need you to put me up on some cash. What's good?" She looked into my eyes, pleading. I took a deep breath.

"Ma, you gotta let me get a few more things in order and I'll put you up on something. But for now, all of them bills you're battling, I'll handle them. I'll take care of Breeyonna, whatever she need just hit my phone. Aight?" She smiled and kissed me on the lips.

"You so one hunnit. Damn, I should have never let yo ass go. Tell Rayven she gon' have to share you, or we gon' have some issues." Though she said it as a joke, I knew she was serious.

102

Chapter 10

I ran into my first problem with the girls about two weeks after the ordeal with Bree. Me and Rayven had just sat down to have a candlelit dinner at her condo in Staten Island when Rabbit showed up, ringing the buzzer to her condo over and over again. Rayven jumped up and ran to the intercom. "Who the hell is it ringing my doorbell like they crazy? I got a license to carry," she warned. She had a real short robe that showed off her golden legs. I had my mind set on getting some of that pussy, but first I wanted to tell her what happened with me and Bree. I wasn't expecting her to have a problem with it, and I was sure she was still doing her thing on the side every now and then. It was more of the fact that I wanted to keep everything on the up and up with her. "Rayven, it's Rabbit, buzz me up. I need your help, it's an emergency."

She finally turned around, so she was facing the camera. She pulled down the Burberry scarf, and exposed her face. Her eyes were wet with tears. Rayven buzzed her up. "Baby, throw a shirt on. I don't want this white bitch lusting all over you right now. I'm trying to see what her issue is and get her the fuck back out of here. Aight?" She looked irritated. I'd been rubbing all over her sexy ass body prior to the doorbell ringing, so I knew she was riled up. Whenever Rayven got riled up and couldn't come, she got real evil, and short with people. I got myself together. From where I was seated on the carpet in front of the fireplace, I could see the screen that showed Rabbit's footage. I got myself together, and grabbed the bottle of Ace of Spades, and sat on the couch with it. Rabbit rushed into the apartment in full tears.

"That son of a bitch caught me, Rayven. He caught me going through his shit and he tried to kill me. Look at my neck. She took the Burberry scarf from around her neck. Rayven flipped on the lights and stepped over to her. Even from the couch, I could see her neck was red and a dark purple. One of her eyes were black and swollen. She came over and sat on the couch across from me. "Hey Kaleb, I didn't know you would be here." Rayven came and sat on the couch beside her and looked over her injuries.

"How did he catch you? Didn't you put the pills in his drink?" Rayven asked, with a face of concern. Rabbit shook her head. "Girl, nall. I didn't get a chance to. That son of a bitch was all over me before I could do anything. We fucked for a long time. I just knew I wore him out. I mean, he was snoring and everything when I went to make my move, but then he woke up. Woke up just as I was copying all his information. I managed to put it all in my phone, but I've paid a terrible price for it. I don't think he knew exactly what I was doing, but he whooped my ass like he did." She handed her phone to Rayven.

Rayven grabbed it and left the room with it. "I'll be right back. She switched out of the room with her big booty jiggling under her robe. I felt a tingle go through my piece. I scooted to the edge of the couch and reached for Rabbit's hand. She jumped back, and then gathered herself. "Oh, you scared the shit out of me." She scooted forward and allowed for me to hold her hands. They were soft. The nails were French tipped.

"Yo, it sucks that he put his hands on you like that, but it's my job to take care of him. Just tell me what you want done and I'll get on it ASAP." She lowered her head.

"I knew what I was getting into when I signed up to do what I've been doing. So far, I've made over a hundred and fifty thousand dollars, not including my new cars, and my condo. I can't complain. I don't want you to do anything crazy. I guess this is supposed to happen." She blinked and tears fell down her cheeks. I stepped past the table and slid on the couch next to her. Put my arm around her shoulders and pulled her into my embrace.

As soon as I did, she broke down crying. Sobbing loudly as I rubbed her back. "It's good, Rabbit. We gon' make him pay. I can't honor nobody putting they hands on my queens. I don't care who they are." I rocked with her just a bit, trying to calm her. She continued to cry. Rayven stepped in the room with a platter of heroin, and a red straw. She sat it on the table in front of us and frowned.

"We don't handle this type of shit like that, Kaleb. You ain't about to go over there waving a fucking gun in a mayor's face. That's not how this works." She pulled Rabbit out of my embrace. "Huh, girl. I got some medicine for you." Rabbit looked up and wiped her tears away. Leaned forward and picked up the straw. Knelt in front of the platter and started to toot a line.

Rayven pulled me away from her and onto the other couch. Once there, she sat on my lap, possessively. "Now, I was able to go through the information that you've gathered and it's good. There are pictures of you and him in here doing the most. And, they are clear. I say we go the blackmail route. He doesn't even have to know you're involved. Kaleb can come off as a jealous boyfriend that found these pictures in your phone. Due to the fact that he's up for re-election, he'll be putty in our hands." She kissed my cheek and laid her face against mine. Rabbit snorted a line hard, and sat on her haunches, pinching her nostrils.

"I don't know. Grant may be the mayor, but he's a tough son of a bitch. I don't think that he'll fold so easily."

"It ain't for you to do the thinking. That's what I'm here for," Rayven said, standing up with her robe high enough to show off her rounded ass. "Just give me a few days with this information, then we'll have Kaleb pay him a visit. Until then, Rabbit, you lay low. No work for you. In fact, you'll stay here with me so we can get your mind right." She knelt on the floor next to her. Stroked her long blonde hair. "You know I'ma take care of you, right?" Kissed her neck and trailed her tongue to her ear.

Rabbit closed her eyes and moaned. I could see traces of the powder on her upper lip. She nodded her head. "Yes. I know you got me, Rayven. You always have." Rayven squeezed her right breast through her Chanel top, before sliding her hand under it, going from one breast, then on to the next. Rayven glanced over at me and smiled. Winked her eye. Rabbit faced Rayven and kissed her lips. "Rayven, what's up with Kaleb? When can I try him out? You said when I bring in two hundred thousand. I've exceeded that already. What's up?" She kissed her lips again, then looked over at me, while Rayven's hands played under her shirt. Rayven slid her tongue into her mouth and shook her head.

"You've been through enough for one night, baby. Let me give you a bath and clean you up real good. Then you'll get some rest, and we'll figure out how we're going to turn this mistake into a cash cow. There will time for Kaleb later. Believe me."

She slid her hand into Rabbit's tight pants, after opening them. Rabbit closed her eyes, and opened them right away, eyeing me through slits. "Okay, baby, but just promise me that he'll fuck me before the other girls. Promise me that and I'm all in." Rayven shook her head.

"Promises are made to be broken, and tomorrow ain't promised to neither one of us. You just keeping earning your way and things will happen when they're supposed to." She grabbed a handful of her hair and yanked her head backward.

Placed her face in front of her ear. "Now, I'm gon' go in here and run your bath water. When I'm finished, bitch, you gon' get in there and soak, until I say you're ready for me to scrub you down. You got that?" She tightened her fingers in her hair.

"Yes, Rayven. Okay, mama." A tear rolled down her cheek. Rayven pushed her away, then stood up, and kissed me on the lips. "You don't cater to these hoes with kindness and emotions. Fuck that. They'll eat your ass alive. You're my nigga, not theirs. You hear me?"

I looked up at her for a short time, before laughing. I grabbed her by the neck, and stood up, took her out of the room and into her bedroom, closing the door. The whole time, she gagged in my hold. I threw her back on the bed and mugged her. "Yo, Rayven, I don't know what you got going with these hoes, but you gon' respect my gangsta or I'ma whoop yo lil ass. You ain't never finna handle me like a simp. Word is bond. Matter fact," I unzipped my pants and pulled my dick out, "top daddy off." My shit was jumping in the air because I was so turned on by how she was handling Rabbit. I loved all that hood shit, especially when it came to a bad ass woman.

"Daddy, you know I was just putting on a good front." She climbed out of the bed, and knelt in front of me, beating my dick back and forth, licking the tip. "You know who run this shit. Them bitches just respond to me. You gotta let me do my thing with them, and we'll be rich. Trust me." She looked up at me with her pretty eyes wide open. I grabbed her head and forced her face into my lap. I needed some relief. I kept imagining how she looked playing with Rabbit's breasts through her shirt. That shit was hot to me. She sucked me hard, twirling her tongue around my head until I came deep down her throat ten minutes later.

* * *

"I'm telling you, Kaleb, this is the only way. I gotta blast this nigga, son. The only time Bree kick me to the curb like she's done is if she's back fucking with this nigga. He got out two weeks ago, and I ain't heard from her since then. Something ain't right." Buddy wiggled his fingers inside of the black leather glove he had on his right hand. We were parked a block away from Ryo's crib. Ryo was Bree's ex, a nigga she usually ran to whenever Buddy and her were on the outs. Buddy acted as if he were sure the two were back messing around, because she wasn't answering any of his calls, and she had him blocked on Facebook. He took this to mean she was shacking up with somebody else. I didn't know if she was fucking back with Ryo or not, and I honestly didn't care. I was more concerned with the welfare of Breeyonna.

"Buddy, even if she.is, you can't go smoke this nigga just because he fucking your B.M. That ain't his fault, it's hers. It takes two." I sat back in the passenger's seat and adjusted the .9 millimeter in my waistband. It was just starting to get dark. The streets were covering with snow. I was tired and had plans on stopping at the hospital so I could check in on my mother. I was missing her and needed to feel her in my arms. She appeared to be getting stronger after undergoing the surgery where they'd removed her right ovary.

"Yo, I don't feel like hearing that shit you got on your mental today, Kaleb. I'ma about to buck this nigga. Now, are you riding with me or not?" he asked in a frustrated tone. As much as I didn't want to, I nodded.

"Yeah, you my nigga. I'm with you. What's good?" I looked behind us and out of the back window for any predators, located none, then looked up at the big project building of the Red Hook Houses. I hated Brooklyn. The niggas in the city were as grimy as they came.

"Yeah, this fuck nigga talking about what he gon' do to me and all that shit when I hit 'em up. Bragging on fucking my Earth. Nah', son, I can't let that shit go down. He should be exiting them doors in the next ten minutes." He nodded with his head to the front entrance of the projects. I blew air out of my jaws and rubbed the palms of my hands on my pants.

"So, when he come out the doors, what's the mission, kid? You gon' just walk up and smoke him?" Buddy snickered.

"Nall, I'ma let the nigga know what it is first, then I'ma put two in his face. Leave his brains all over the sidewalk. I'm talking big pieces of his noodles. Word up." I nodded.

"Aight." I took my black mask, and put it on top of my head as if it were just a skull cap. I didn't wanna be fucking around wit Buddy on this dumb ass mission, but I felt guilty for getting his hand chopped off, and for fucking his Earth behind his back. Not only was she his Earth, but she was the mother of his daughter. It sucked that her pussy was so good. A nice tight, wet fit. I still thought about it on occasion. Buddy, tapped my shoulder as the doors to the project opened and Ryo stepped out of it, holding a little girl in his arms.

"Yo money, if that's my daughter, on my mother, I'm killing Bree." Buddy promised. I felt sick to my stomach when I glanced over to the front of the building and I saw Ryo sit a little girl down on her feet while he helped her with her pink scarf. I couldn't tell if it was Breeyonna or not, but I was praying it wasn't. I knew Buddy would kill Bree in cold blood with no hesitation. He was nuts like that. Out the window, Ryo finished helping the little girl get ready for the cold, then he picked her up and made his way toward the parking lot, just as the snow started to fall. As soon as they stepped under one of the street lamps in the parking lot, I was able to make out Breeyonna's face, and I knew it was on.

"Fuck," I muttered. Buddy threw open the door to the Jeep we were sitting in and slid his hand under his shirt. Jogged across the sidewalk and headed for the parking lot in pursuit of them. I opened the passenger's door, and slid my mask down at the same time, chasing behind him. "Hold up, bruh. Damn," I hollered into the night.

Buddy was in a zone of his own. He rushed in front of Ryo and pointed his gun in his face. "Bitch-ass nigga, if you don't drop my muthafuckin' daughter, I'ma splatter yo shit all over this parking lot. Put her down!" he spat, neglecting to have worn a mask. I caught up to him with my chest burning. The cold air was taking my breath away. My nose felt frozen already. Ryo frowned, and looked at me running up, and his eyes got big.

"Yo, you coming at me over a bitch? I'm out here doing yo job, and this how you repay me?" he asked, with smoke rising from his mouth. His nose was red on his yellow face. Breeyonna heard Buddy's voice and turned all the way around in Ryo's arms. "Daddy. I want my daddy. I want my daddy," she cried, reaching out for Buddy. Ryo jerked her back.

"Yo, you can have lil shorty, just put the gun down, kid. I was doing Bree a favor, so she could go to work. That's all. We ain't fucking a nothing like that."

Buddy stepped closer. "Nigga, put my daughter down, or I'm about to splatter you." He cocked the hammer and turned the gun sideways. His nostrils flared. I could see his soul leave his eyes. Within them was nothing but death. Ryo looked from me, back to Buddy.

"Alright, man." He took a deep breath, then out of nowhere, he threw Breeyonna as hard as he could into Buddy's face and took off running. The little girl crashed into his face, then fell to the floor on her head. Took a deep breath and started to scream. Instead of Buddy reaching down to pick her up, he took off running behind Ryo, bussing. *Boo-wa! Boo-wa! Boo-wa!* His gunshots echoed in the night. he scent of the gun powder heavy in the air. I knelt and picked Breeyonna from the ground. I could see a large gash on the side of her face. Blood ran from it. I stood up and rocked her while she screamed.

"Baby, it's okay. It's okay. I'm here. You're alright. You're alright." I kissed her warm cheek and held her more firmly to my chest. She was hysterical.

I looked up and saw Ryo fall to the ground. Buddy rushed and stood over him, bussing his gun. *Boo-wa! Boo-wa! Boo-wa! Boo-wa!* He kicked his body three times in the midsection, then bussed him five more times. The snow turned red all around his body. He stood looking down at Ryo, before jogging back over to me, looking both ways. "Let's get out of here, kid, give me my seed." I handed him Breeyonna. Her screaming stopped. It dwindled to only a whimper. The gash in her forehead constantly bled. We jumped into the Jeep, and I stormed away from the curb.

"Yo, son, you're nuts. How the fuck you gon' explain what happened to Bree? Shorty about to be out of her mind!" I hollered, looking in my rearview mirror at this nigga.

"Fuck that bitch, B. Punk-ass bitch got another nigga carrying my seed. To the dirt wit her, Blood. On my mother!" Breeyonna started to scream in his arms. "Mommy! Mommy. I want my mommy!" She started to shake.

"Blood, I know you're vexed, but that's still your B.M. You can't whack shorty just like she's some average nigga in the hood. Nall, that's her mother, son. Think about it."

"Man, Kaleb, I love you kid. But word to my mother, if you keep on trying to kick knowledge, I'ma blow at you. Fuck that bitch. When I catch her, I'm icing her. To the freezer wit her, son!" I mugged him in my rearview mirror and nodded.

"Yeah aight, Blood. Not my bidness. Do ya thing. I'ma roll back to my whip and be out of your hair."

Chapter 11

"Baby, it's been two weeks and I've been on his ass. Rocking him from every angle. All you gotta do is have a sit-down with him and y'all will get an understanding. You're going under the pretense of being Rabbit's scorned lover. He knows you have all of the pictures. All the text messages, and info that only somebody close to him could have. All of the odds are in our favor. He's running for reelection. He can't have any stains on his record, because he's only up by a few points in the polls. So, trust me, he'll be willing to play ball. Our goal is a few million. We'll take half in cash, and half in property. It doesn't matter, just as long as it adds up at the end of the day. You get me?" Rayven asked, sipping out of her wine glass. She looked into my eyes. Behind her, Rabbit crawled across the bed with her gown around her waist. Her bald, pink pussy on full display. The lips looked engorged, and plump.

I dusted off my Armani suit, and straightened my tie. "Yeah, I got you. I know how to handle this stud. I been looking over the blueprints and listening to your recorded phone calls with him." I faced the mirror and made sure I was looking as confident as I was feeling. My head was spinning like a top.

"He don't like niggas, Kaleb. Be careful," Rabbit said in a strained voice. She laid on her back and opened her thick white thighs, showing me her gash. She trailed her fingers through the lips and opened them for me. The pink looked shiny. I groaned deep within my throat. I had never been with a white girl before, but her lil thick ass could get it. Rayven snapped her neck and turned around to scold her.

"Bitch, I told you about saying that nigga shit. Just 'cuz you built like a sista, don't mean you are one." She turned

113

back to me. "Kaleb, just be smart, and make sure you keep our best interest at heart. I trust you." She stepped forward and wrapped her arms around my neck.

I looked back at the bed. Rabbit flickered her tongue at me. Slid two fingers into herself, ran them in and out, then mouthed the words, "I wanna fuck you so bad." Her tongue ran all over her juicy lips. Both her nipples poked through her tiny wife beater. I felt my dick getting hard. I took a step back from Rayven before she could feel it. The room smelled like perfume and pussy. The perfect combination. "Yo, I got this. I'll be back in a few hours."

* * *

"Kaleb, I bet you never been in a helicopter before, have you?" Mayor Grant asked as he adjusted his cuff links. He looked over to me and smiled, then looked out of the big window. His words came through distorted on the head set that I was wearing.

"Nall, I only been in the air one time. That was when I was younger, and my mother took me on a trip to Haiti. One day, flying in a chopper is going to be a normal thing for me. I can feel it." The chopper flew past the Statue of Liberty, and over the water. Snow fell from the sky in light patches. It smelled like Mennen Speed Stick all around and I didn't know why that was.

"And I supposed when you envision this chopper, you imagine you'll be using my money to purchase it?" He snickered. Mayor Grant was a heavy-set white man, with a red face, and double chin.

I could tell he was cocky by his demeanor. He carried himself like he was filthy with cash and used to getting his way. I didn't like him one bit. He reminded me of a slave master from the movies. I wanted to spit in his face. "Only a fool would use his own money to purchase something as high-priced as this. I'm pretty sure that's why you use taxpayer money." I laughed at my own slickness. He looked over at me and smiled.

"I come from a long line of men that used others to do the work for them. They break their backs, and we reap the benefits. It's the American Way." He curled his lip and looked back out of the window. "What are you expecting to accomplish here today, Kaleb? I hope you have a nice game plan, because I'm ready to play chess." The helicopter cruised over the harbor. The whirring of the blades made the water go in scattered waves. From the view, I could see a nice portion of the city. I felt it was how a boss was supposed to roll.

"Where are we headed, Grant?" I had yet to find that out.

"The Hamptons. I wanna show you a nice time. There, we'll come to an understanding that will make both sides happy. I'm sure of it." He snapped his fingers, and a real pretty white woman, dressed like a stewardess in a Prada uniform, handed me a cigar and a small vial of cocaine. I took both of them and set them on the small table that was in front of me.

"I ain't come to be swindled, Grant. I got money on my mind, and I ain't talking crumbs. Tell this bitch to fall back, unless she ready to offer me some of the fields this cocaine was taken from." He turned in his seat and looked back at her and laughed.

"Well, she can't offer you none of that, but she can give you some of the best damn head of your life. How 'bout it?" The white girl balanced herself in the aisle and knelt in front of me, licking her lips.

"Can I? I never sucked a black one before. I hear they're all the raves." I muffed her with my right hand.

"And, you still ain't. Yo, tell this bitch to put on her seat belt." Mayor Grant started to laugh and grabbed her by the hair, tossing her into the door of the chopper. "Kaleb, I see you're going to be a thorn in my side."

* * *

I grabbed the bottle of Moet out of the bucket of ice and popped the cork. Took a long swallow and burped. Placed it next to my plate packed with a nice, juicy well-done steak, a baked potato, corn, and sour cream. I'd already eaten half of the steak and it was fire. I used the champagne to wash it down. Grant sat at the other end of the long table, smoking tobacco out of his peace pipe. He blew a big cloud of smoke into the air and smiled down at me. "So, what do you want?"

I ate the meat from my fork. "Tell me what you are you offering and we'll go from there."

He scooted his chair back and stood up. The room was decorated with all kinds of British war paintings. A crystal chandelier hung from the ceiling. "Before we discuss any of that, let me tell you what I know about you. The first thing. I know you're nothing more than a two-bit Harlem hustler. You've never held a job for more than a month. You finished high school last year, applied to college, but never stepped foot inside of one, even though you spent the financial aid."

"You don't know your father, but I do. And, your mother is in Mount Sinai Hospital, fighting the disease of cervical cancer. She has no insurance, no money and no chance, unless there is a change in circumstances. Am I correct so far?" To say I was getting mad was an understatement. I didn't like how this white man had picked me apart so easily. He'd done his homework. It was something I should have expected.

"Yeah, well you do work for the government, and what? I'm supposed to be impressed or something?" I took a sip from the Moet and burped as loud as I could. His smile turned into a frown. "What?"

"Let me tell you what I know about you. You're up for re-election and right now, you're only ahead in the polls by three points. You're married to a woman that comes from a rich background. She's the one that gave you the in to the social world here in New York. The reason you were able to become mayor. You've cheated on her before, and she was seconds away from leaving yo ass, but somehow you convinced her to stay and things have been rocky ever since then. You have a thing for your daughter, and every time you screwed Rabbit, you had her dress in your daughter, Tabitha's, clothing and act as if she was her. The footage is sickening. All of this centers on you remaining mayor of the city, as soon as you lose that seat, you'll lose everything. Especially if you go out how I'm predicting you will." I laughed and ate another piece of my steak. The Armani suit had me a little sweaty, but I was braving the elements. Grant came within five feet of me and stopped.

"Son of a bitch, what is your end game?" He slammed his right hand on the table. I saw that it was full of rings. I cut another piece of my steak and chewed it nice and slow. Swallowed and wiped my mouth on a napkin. "First of all, I want my mother moved to the best hospital in New York City. I'm talkin' about one where the doctors are wizards." I looked up to him.

"That's done. I'll make sure that she gets cared for as if she's the first lady of the United States. You have my word. What else?"

"Money? At least a few million. No less than three. Can you swing that?" He ran his fingers through his hair and scratched his scalp.

"I'll have to move some things around, but I'm sure it can be arranged. What's your deadline for this cash?"

"Yesterday." I sucked my teeth and picked at a piece of meat that was stuck in the back in my wisdom teeth. He paced back and forth and started to sweat.

"I don't know how I got caught up with that whore. I knew she was rotten. Now, I'm screwed. Screwed, unless..." He stopped midstride and smiled. "Wait a minute. You're from Harlem, right?" I wiped my mouth on a napkin and sat back in my leather seat. I felt like a boss having this white man run back and forth like a chicken with its head cut off.

"Yeah, and what about it?" He pulled out a chair and took a seat. Wiped sweat from his forehead.

"You've been a hussler all your life. What would you say if I helped you to advance a little further, swifter in the game you know so well? What would you say to that?"

"I'd say I'm interested. Explain yourself, Mayor." He stood up.

"You're not an idiot. I'm sure that you can look at New York and tell what's going on here. The city is full of haves and have-nots. The haves are haves because of you have-nots." He grabbed the bottle of Moet and drank out of it. That meant I wasn't fucking wit it no more. Not only would I never drink behind any man, but definitely not his red-faced ass. He looked gross to me. Sweaty as hell.

"Speak plain language, Grant. Don't be trying to talk over my head and shit."

"Kaleb, there is a design in place for your people to fail at all costs. Every mayor, every governor, every politician is given this game plan directly after they are sworn into office.

It is by design that your people remain at the bottom of the totem pole. In order for our nation to prosper, there has to be a race of people on the bottom. The game plan says that all we need is one, but here in New York, we use two. Both blacks and Latinos. You are the trash of our civilization." A part of me wanted to jump out of my seat and attack his ass. But then, another part of me wanted to hear him out. I knew what he was saying could be useful for me for the long term.

"Go on." I balled my fists under the table.

"Divide, destroy, and conquer. Those are the rules and the key to privileged white men like me staying in power. Every man in power must have a key slave sort of speak that keeps the other slaves in order. One that reports everything back to his master. One the master treats better than all the rest. One the other slaves will aspire to be like but will never get the opportunity. Donald Trump has Kanye West, and me, Mayor Jeffery Grant, I'll have you. You will be put above all the rest, if you're willing to play ball." He was hitting me with one heavy slug after the next. I was so mad my vision was going blurry, but I needed to see where he was going with things. I was thirty-two too now. "I want you to help me flood Harlem and Brooklyn with Fentanyl and heroin. The best quality a man can get. If you'll do this and dispose of all of the material you have on me. I'll see to it that your mother is well taken care of. And that you become a filthy rich man for as long as I am in office.

"You will have no worries on the law enforcement side of things. Your shipments will come from untapped sources in both China and Vietnam. That's my word. But, you have to play ball, and you'll only flood the areas that you are appointed to destroy. Any other places will be outside of your jurisdiction. You get that? You're not the only slave out there. No kingpin can become a kingpin without the go-ahead from the other powers that be. Everything you see on the surface is only possible because of what you cannot see, if that makes any sense?"

It did. "Yo, I don't like you calling me a slave and all of that shit. I'm a man. My people ain't been slaves for hundreds of years now." I was getting irritated sitting in front of that white man, hearing him talk about me and my race of people like we were nothing more than trash. Asking me to destroy them with an utter lack of regard. He shrugged his shoulders.

"Kaleb, 'kid', isn't that the expression that you inner-city citizens use? Well, kid, your people have never been free, and as long as America exists, they never will be. Out of all of the races on earth, the black race is the most athletically powerful. The strongest. The most well-built from the inside out, yet mentally, it is the weakest and the easiest to enslave and control. You guys hate yourselves more than you hate your oppressors. You're too busy trying to compete with and fight each other. We can't imagine what unity looks like in your race, so we don't fear you. You are a divided house. With your different color skin tones, and class distinctions, you find reasons within yourselves to hate the one that looks just like you. All we do is feed into your own self destruction." He laughed and started to pace.

"Don't look at me as if I'm the enemy, Kaleb. Like you, I'm just dealing the hand that I was dealt. It's about survival. The game is to win by any means. Nothing lasts forever. You can either live happily in this life, or miserable. I am extending you an olive branch. If you are willing to work with me, I'll make you rich, and help to cure your mother of her sickness. If not, we can go to war, and both lose. The only difference between you and I are our skin complexions, race, and bank account balances. So, you do the math. In the end, who do you think will fare better?" He picked up a glass of champagne and took a sip from it. I sat back in the chair and stared at the chandelier that hung from the ceiling, replaying over everything that he'd said about my people. I wanted to dive deeper into the conversation, to pick his brain, to get insider information. I wanted to hear about the design. For him to open my eyes.

I was hungry for knowledge. I'd been a project misfit my whole life. Never had a mentor, or anybody that opened my third eye the way he had in just a few short minutes. I felt like I had to do something. I had to break the mold. I couldn't fall victim or allow those I loved to fall either. I was so confused, and hungry for knowledge, that I felt angry. He came and stood to the left of me.

"So, what is it going to be, Kaleb? Are you going to play ball? Allow for me to take you out of your circumstances and in exchange, be what I need for you to be?" I stood up and pressed my forehead to his.

"I ain't nobody's slave, Grant. I'm free. I'll never let you Yankees enslave me." I bumped him out of my way and headed toward the door with murder on my mind. I needed to kill something. Needed to do something to release myself from this anger I was feeling. The anger of my reality.

"Think about your mother. Your precious and beautiful mother. Don't you know that those doctors don't give a fuck because of what the computer says about her? She's poor. Broke. Their job is to give her the minimum care as possible. Nobody cares about a broke, black woman in America. Nobody other than her children."

He slammed his hand on the table so hard that it knocked the bottle of champagne over. "Get your head out of your own ass and save her at the very least. And your slave comment, sooner or later, you'll wind up on the plantation of prison. It's by design that you do. You are nothing more than a nigger in the eyes of America. You are America's nigger. Not mine. Now, I can guarantee you a new life. Destroy and get rich, or run away and stay poor, it's your choice."

Chapter 12

Bree rushed into my arms and hugged me tight with tears running down her cheeks. She shook against my body. "I don't know what to do, Kaleb. He has my daughter and he says that he's not giving her back unless I come to get her myself. I'm so scared. I know he killed Ryo. He told me he did. I can't go to the police. Then, he'll kill Breeyonna. And I can only imagine what he'll do to me. I need your help. I'll do anything. Just please help me to get my baby back. Please." She cried and sunk to her knees until her face was against my thighs. I knelt on the floor next to her and wrapped my arm around her shoulders. I didn't like to see women cry. Especially, those I cared about. I didn't know what was going on with Buddy. It had been two weeks since he'd killed Ryo, and he'd not returned any of my calls. I was worried about him, but Breeyonna even more so. She was four years old now, and her father was strung out on heroin.

I couldn't understand how would be able to manage a habit like that while caring for a baby girl. It had me going out of my mind. I kissed the side of Bree's forehead with a heavy heart. "I got you, ma. I'll do all that I can but stand up. I don't like seeing you down like you are." I pulled her up, and she reluctantly came to a standstill with her shoulders hunched inward. The shaking continued. I lead her to the couch and set her down. We were at her small apartment. It looked a mess, like she hadn't cleaned it in a few days.

"Kaleb, ever since my daughter has been gone, I haven't been able to think straight, or eat anything. I'm sick. I don't know what to do." She broke down again, and buried her face into my big chest, sobbing loudly. I rubbed her back.

"Yo, I'm about to go over to where I know he's laying his head and talk some sense into him. But you know you was bogus for having that nigga, Ryo, babysitting his daughter. That was foul, ma. I expect more from you than that."

"I caught eight hours from a temp service on some ushering shit. I had to go right away. We needed that money. Ryo was in the building. I asked him if he'd watch her until I got off work. That was all it was. Me and him wasn't fucking around or none of that. I don't know what Buddy was talking about." I stood up.

"Still, you don't have your ex watching Blood's kid. You knew that wouldn't blow over well. But, now ain't the time to cry over spilled milk. I'ma go over here and try and rectify the situation. You know he still trying to fuck wit you tho, right?" She lowered her face into her hands and rocked back and forth.

"I don't want to think about that right now, Kaleb. I hate this man. I never want to be with him again. I just want my daughter back, that's all." She broke down again. I grabbed her hair and pulled her head back. Kissed her forehead and smiled down at her.

"I got you, Bree, just chill. Matter fact get dressed, you're rolling over here with me."

She looked up at me in horror. "Nall, Kaleb. I can't. That fool said he was gon' kill me when he caught me, and I believe him. If I go over there with you, he's going to shoot me. There will be nothing you can do about it."

"Bree, get ya ass up, and get dressed. I said you're rolling over here with me, don't make that me say that shit again. Come on," I demanded. She stood in front of me and took a deep breath.

"You got me, right?" Her eyes searched mine for sincerity. I could sense her apprehension. She knew like I knew that Buddy was crazy. The fact that he had been

124

beating her ever since they'd been together didn't help matters any. I didn't know how he was going to react, but I would protect Bree as best I could. The man in me wouldn't allow for him to hurt her. I pulled her to me and hugged her frame.

"Yeah, I got you, ma. Just get dressed so we can roll out."

* * *

The sun peaked from behind the clouds, as a light breeze brushed across my back. It was about fifty degrees outside, and better than it had been over the past few weeks. There were big snow banks that were melting. The roads were covered in salt and sand. Birds flew overhead chirping along. Empty branches rustled in the trees behind me, which were in front of the Super 8 Motel I knew Buddy was staying in. Every time we'd had to lay low, he went to the same motel, and copped the same room if it were available. The owners were so used to him coming, they tried their best to keep the room that he rented on a regular basis unoccupied, until he rented it out, usually no more than a week after he'd left it. I balled my fist and beat on the door for the second time. This time, harder. Bree stood on the side of the door looking both ways. Shaking. I could tell that she was scared out of her mind, and at the same time optimistic she was about to see Breeyonna again. "Yo, who the fuck is it? My word, I'm about to start shooting through the door," came Buddy's voice on the other side.

"Nigga shut up, and open the damn door," I ordered, and beat on it again. I heard the locks clicking, and then the door slowly swung inward. I was expecting it to open all the way, but he stopped it short.

"Yo, what you want, Kaleb? I ain't fucking wit nobody right now. I'm on a mountain, kid." In Harlem, whenever we said that we were on a mountain, we were saying that we were off into the deepest regions of our minds. We wanted to be alone to find ourselves. In the Bible, whenever God wanted to reveal something life altering to the prophets, he took them up on a mountain, and showed them the light. Gave them ultimate wisdom. Buddy was basically telling me that he was trying to find himself. "Blood, we need to squash this shit between you and Bree. Y'all gotta get an understanding, for Breeyonna's sake. Nah' mean?" He shook his head.

"Nah' B. I'm stanking that bitch. I can't believe she'd have some nigga she was fucking watching my seed. I can't honor, nor forgive her for that. I gotta knock that spaghetti out of her head. That's all I see, kid. Fuck everything else." Bree's eyes got big as saucers on the side of the door. She looked like she wanted to run away, and I couldn't blame her from how he was talking.

"Nah', it ain't gon' be none of that. Let's squash this shit, B. Let me in." I bumped into the door and nudged it all the way open. Breeyonna was laying in the bed and when she saw me, she opened her little arms, and reached out for me. Buddy took a deep breath and frowned.

"Yo, I said I'm on a mountain, kid. Damn," he snapped.

"Aight, now listen. Buddy, I need you to hear me out. Don't do no fucking snapping. Bree is here. We all about to sit down and get an understanding, that's all. You gon' leave her pasta inside her head, and we gon' act like civilized adults. Cool?" His eyes got big.

"That bitch here? Where?" He rushed toward the door, trying to knock me out of the way. Now, I was irritated. I pushed his ass back into the room.

"Nigga, chill. Sit yo ass down on the bed by Breeyonna. I ain't finna play these games today. Straight up."

He mugged me for a few seconds, then nodded his head. "Yeah, aight, B. Bring her in. I ain't on shit. But she better have a damn good excuse for having that fuck nigga babysit my daughter. I ain't playing neither." He plopped on the bed and picked up Breeyonna, kissing her cheek. I stepped outside, and waved Bree over.

"Come on, Bree, its good. I ain't gon' let the homie hurt you," I promised. She bit on her fingernail, and slowly made her way to me, until she was standing in the doorway. I placed my arm around her shoulders and stepped into the room with her.

"Mama! Mama!" Breeyonna screamed and tried to jump out of Buddy's arms. Buddy held her, preventing her from breaking loose.

"Calm down, lil girl. Chill," he hollered.

"I wanna see my daughter." Bree rushed to the bed and tried to pry his arms away from Breeyonna, with no success.

"Yo, get this bitch or I'ma fuck her up, Kaleb. That's my word," he said through clenched teeth. Bree broke into a fit of tears, still trying to get his arms loose. After seeing that she couldn't win the struggle, she settled for kissing all over Breeyonna's face. "I love you, baby. I love you so much."

Buddy raised his wrist, and back-handed her so hard, he bussed her nose. Then, he flung his daughter across the bed. She crashed into the headboard and started to scream for Bree. Bree fell against me, before falling on to her knees. Blood gushed out of her nostrils.

"Why, Buddy? Why?"

"You a ho, bitch. Fucking niggas and leaving my daughter wit 'em. I'ma kill you." He upped a pistol out of his waist so fast, it caught me off guard. He pressed the barrel to

Bree's face. "If I can't have you, then nobody can." He cocked the hammer.

I tackled him as hard as I could. The gun went off. We crashed into the lamp table. The Bible and television remote control fell onto the carpet. He tussled against me, holding the gun in his hand. "Let me go, Kaleb. I'm finna kill that bitch. I'm finna kill that bitch, B. I'm tired of that bitch doing me wrong. Fuck she think this is?" Bree rushed to the bed with her nose dripping blood, grabbed Breeyonna, then took off out of the room. She fell at the door on both knees, got up and ran with her daughter.

"Nigga, chill. I ain't finna let you kill your baby mother. Are you crazy?"

He brought his knee to my nuts, catching me off guard again. The pain was so intense, that I threw up in my mouth and rolled off of him, holding my shits. He scrambled to his feet with the gun in his hand. Got to the doorway and stepped out of it, looked in the direction that Bree had run with Breeyonna and fired. *Boom. Boom.* Then, took off running behind her. I had to fight through the pain. I flipped onto my knees and got up, running behind him with my gun out. "Buddy! No!" I hollered in a strained voice. It felt like my balls were in my stomach, and my stomach was in my mouth. When I got outside, Buddy was at the top of the stairs, getting ready to run down them. He stopped, aimed over the banister downward and fired again. *Boom. Boom.*

"Fuck. Punk-ass bitch. Ah! I'ma kill that bitch!" He started walking back my way with a mug on his face. "You ain't got no kids, Kaleb, I don't want to hear your mouth right now." He bumped me and acted as if he'd not just tried to kill both his baby mother and his child. I was seriously starting to think Buddy was losing his mind.

I didn't know if it was the drugs that he was doing, or if he'd given up on life altogether ever since his hand had been cut off. I couldn't help but to feel guilty. I looked around to see if anybody was looking out of their windows, but didn't see anything out of the ordinary. This area of Harlem was so bad the residents probably took it as a normal day in the hood. No biggie. I followed Buddy into his room. When I got in there, he was sittin' on the bed with his gun in his right hand. The tip of the barrel looked tarnished. I imagined because it was still hot. "Yo, you fucking up, kid. You fucking all the way up. What if you would have hit one of them?" I snapped. He looked at me with anger.

"Nigga, that's what I was trying to do. That was my whole point of aiming at her punk ass and blasting. Damn!" He hopped up. "I can't see her being with no other nigga, Kaleb. I'd rather kill that bitch, than to allow that. I'm serious. I love that girl way too much, and you already know how I feel about my baby. Fuck the world if I ain't the head of them, kid. Word up." He slid his arms into the sleeves of his Gucci jacket. "I gotta get the fuck out of here. I need a fix too. I feel sick and shit." He wiped his nose.

I dug in my pocket and tossed him about a quarter-ounce of heroin. A supply sample that one of Grant's connects had hit me up with a few days prior. "Yo, get right, money, and let me holler at you." The dope landed on the bed. He picked it up with his eyes bucked. Smacked his lips and sat back down, wiggled his arms out of his coat, and grabbed his works from the night table.

"Man, you been holding out? You getting down too or what?" He started to get the dope prepared to be shot.

"Nah', son. I'm clean, but I'm giving you this shit, because I need you to holler at me. Can you do that?" He continued to do his thing, nodded his head while tying a rope around his left bicep. I was surprised at how he did everything so easily as if the hand had not been missing to begin with. "Yeah, I'll hear you out."

I waited until he was seconds away from shooting the poison, then got at him. "Son, what do you want to do with your life? Can you see past Harlem?" I asked, feeling defeated. I wondered if I could really see outside of it myself.

"Yo, I'm just trying to make it out of today. I already know I ain't got no future. It's meant for niggas like us to fall flat on our faces, kid. And I have. Fuck it. This is the Big Apple, where niggas get hung just like 'em." He pushed the heroin into his system, His eyes rolled into the back of his head. He ran his tongue across his lips and sunk to the floor from the bed. I looked down at him and shook my head.

"I ain't about to accept that fate, Blood. I ain't finna be the average project nigga. The average low-life. I'ma about to buss up out of here, and be great, and I'm taking my people with me. I wanna go to college, son. One of them black universities so I can learn more in depth about where we come from. I feel ignorant, Buddy, I don't like feeling like this. I wanna conquer the conquerors. Make the white man my slave. I know I can do it, I just gotta think outside of the box."

Buddy slowly made his way back to the bed and sat back against the headboard. His eyes were low. A slight trace of drool leaked from the corner of his mouth. "You ain't step on this shit, Kaleb. You supposed to step on it a little bit."

He slid down until he was laying in the bed, fucked up. The heroin was ninety-eight percent pure. I hadn't stepped on it. I was expecting a shipment of a hundred kilos of that product by the end of the week. "Yo, do ya thing, Buddy, and I'll be back for you. I'ma get some other shit in order, then I'ma clean you up. You about to ball hard, baby. Trust me. We finna break out of New York, but first we take over our slums. It's all about the legacy now. Being more than what they expect us to be. You hear me?" Buddy continued to slob. His eyes were blank. He closed them and smiled.

"I hear you, Kaleb."

I sat there watching him for a long time, feeling worse than I had before. He represented what so many of our people were going to look like once I destroyed them, in order to get to the top of the mountain, so I could destroy the powers at the top of it. I was on a focused mission. I wanted my last name to mean something more than what it did thus far. I wanted to be great. To be a legend. To change the world as I knew it, before I slept with the maggots. So, before I had ever told Mayor Grant I would accept his offer, I made my mind up to right there in Buddy's room, while he went through the transformations the heroin was taking him through.

T.J. Edwards

Chapter 13

In a matter of two months, I had Brooklyn up and rocking with the finest heroin that the city had ever gotten ahold of. Every kilo was laced with an ounce of pure Fentanyl from Hong Kong. Buddy had cousins plugged into the Red River Houses in Brooklyn, and I had some extended family that were connected in Bed-Stuy. All it took was for me to offer them a kilo off of every three they sold and we were on and rocking. The heroin was so pure that the fiends couldn't get enough of it. They lined up all around the building single-file, waiting to cop their shares, while the homies kept the lines in order and served them accordingly. Every time I made a trip to Brooklyn, I felt out of place. I didn't give a fuck that the niggas we were doing business with were supposed to be related and close to us. I personally didn't trust the gods out in Brooklyn. They were some of the sheistiest niggas in the city to me. So, I kept my third eye opened at all times, and made Buddy the overseer of all Brooklyn affairs.

I didn't really trust him either, but he was the only one I could depend on outside of myself to deal with those clowns. Long as the numbers added up, I was good to go. Grant had a certain area designated for me to build my operations on. The law enforcement had been put in tune with what was taking place and fell in line, but that didn't stop me from greasing their palms from time to time with hefty sums of money. I figured that as long as I kept them burping and well-fed, I wouldn't have much to worry about. They went from looking at me from the corners of their eyes, to calling me Mister. That shit felt weird. I was only a few months into my new journey. I had this thing where I liked to watch things from a distance. I took the information that I gathered from watching the hustlers work and used it to develop strategies to help the operations flow more smoothly. No area was the same. Each project was different, because there was always some group of niggas that thought they owned that turf, when in reality, the ones that held the dope and money owned everybody in that community one way or the other. I understood that you learned more from observing than you did actually being in the middle of things.

Rayven came to me four months after I got to grinding with a big smile on her face. She took my hand and placed it on her stomach after coming out of the bathroom in my condo. "Kaleb, guess what, honey? Guess what?" she asked, excited. I was just waking up. Had been out all night, popping bottles with Buddy. Somehow, some way, Bree had come back to him and he felt the need to celebrate. I didn't know what had convinced her to have a change of heart, or what she was thinking, but the homie was happy and I was there to support him. He'd made his first hundred thousand dollars in addition to Bree's return. I was happier about that than anything else, because in order for him to make a hundred thousand, that meant I'd made one fifty. So, all was well. I sat up and wiped the cold out of my eyes.

"What's good, baby?"

"Daddy, I'm pregnant. I'm pregnant with our child. Isn't that amazing?" she shrieked and threw her arms around my neck.

I hugged her, shocked. I was happy, but at the same time, I didn't know if I was really ready to raise a child. There was so much work to be done. I had so much to learn. The game was still fresh to me. I didn't know how many enemies I had, but I knew there were many. Grant assured me of that. He'd told me he couldn't control my beefs. That was on me. The only things he could control were the drugs, flow ways, and the law. That was it. But, I had enough common sense to know that whenever a new player stepped foot into the game, he became public enemy number-one, especially if his dope was as good as the shit I was getting.

"Baby, when did you find this out?" I asked, looking up at her.

"Just a few minutes ago. I peed on two sticks. They both came back positive." She looked me over closely. "Why, aren't you happy?" She frowned and smacked my hands away. "Oh, my God, you aren't. You look pissed. Really?" She started to walk away from me. I slipped out of the bed and caught her in the middle of the floor. She had the big curtains pulled backward, exposing the sun and the ocean that her window overlooked.

It appeared that it would be a hot spring day. I had yet to cop me a whip for the heat. But I thought that today would be the day. Why not? My arms circled around her body. "Get away from me, Kaleb. I can't believe that look you just gave me. You hurt my feelings," she snapped angrily, trying to break away from me. I held her tighter from the back. Kissed the side of her face.

"Chill, baby. I'm very happy. I always knew you was going to be the mother of my child. Who else but you?" I added, kissing her again. She felt so soft, and now that she had my seed growing inside of her, she really made me feel some type of way. She turned to face me.

"Are you serious? You're really happy?" I slid my hands down and cuffed her big booty, gripping it.

"Shorty, wit all this money you making, I needed to find a way to lock yo ass down. Now I got tabs on this temple for the next eighteen years. Lucky me. Gimme some." I kissed her soft lip and slid my tongue into her mouth.

She kissed me for a brief second, then pushed me away. "Get off of me. Then, why did you look at me like that at first?" Poked her bottom lip out, acting like a little girl. I thought she looked cute in that role. It was exactly how she used to act when we were little. Brought back memories.

"It was the first thing I heard when I opened my eyes, baby. It took me a few seconds to process what you were even talking about. That's all." I pulled her back to me. "Don't sweat the small things. We gotta come up with a plan to shield you from the everyday stresses in life. You gotta deliver us a healthy baby. Nah' mean." She pushed me away.

"Nigga get off of me. I just told you I'm pregnant and the first thing you think about is shielding me from business? You should be carrying your ass out to Jacob the Jeweler and getting me an engagement ring. I'm a queen. I'm not bringing your kid into this world without a ring on my finger. What you got to say about that?" She crossed her arms in front of her perfect frame. I couldn't do nothing but laugh. I stepped forward and took her back into my arms.

"Then, that's what it is. We'll make that official tonight after a nice dinner. I already know you thinking pink lemonade, am I right?" She nodded.

"Yeah, you know me well. I want this ring looking like a house of mirrors. I'm a diamond, so you gotta treat me as such."

* * *

That night we sat down in front of a full course meal at Escobar's. Escobar's was in the top three restaurants in New York's upper Manhattan. So exclusive that you had to book your reservations months in advance and even then, they weren't promised if you weren't in the proper social outfit.

Lucky for me, I was plugged with the mayor of the city and so far, business was good. To his knowledge, he'd been given back all of the evidence against him, and we were on eye level terms. He'd already had my mother moved to a top-notch treatment center in the Hamptons. A four-star general's wife was being treated there, too. I felt confident, and secure.

In his eyes, there was no reason for me to cross him. And, even though he'd held up his word thus far, I had duplicates of everything that was to be used against him when the time was right. I had a timer in my head for our relationship. I knew it couldn't last too long. I needed to get in and get out of it. Like he'd said before, the slave master never really cared about the slave. The slave was nothing more than a pawn in the grand scheme of things.

After we enjoyed a delicious meal, Rayven slid her hand across the table and took ahold of mine. Her index finger danced over the yellow-faced Rolex watch that Grant had given me as a gift for the new year. "Baby, I'm so happy right now. It feels good to not have any worries. Am I right? I mean, your mother is in Washington Medical, getting the best treatment that money can buy. Money that we don't even have to supply. The girls are kicking ass on their hustles. You're killing the game with what you're doing. Your siblings are straight. You've enrolled in college. I mean, it's just online but it's a major step, nonetheless. I just got my real estate license. Shouldn't we be happy?" she asked, staring deeply into my eyes. I smiled and nodded. The place was packed. A soft Frank Sinatra song bellowed from the speakers. The waiters went from table to table, with a white towel draped over their arms. There was a strong scent of mint in the air. The other patrons looked like rich, stuck-up people. I could tell by their mannerisms that they were privileged.

"Baby, I want more than what we have. I know we're just getting started, but I see where I want to be and it's frustrating me."

She looked concerned. "What's the matter, baby? Talk to me." I shook my head.

"I don't know. I just feel like I gotta do something, and I don't know what I gotta do. I want to change the world, or something. Flip it upside down. I'm ready to rub elbows with the upper echelon. Tired of being in the basement." I exhaled and continued to look around. She raised her left eyebrow.

"Are you sure you're not on nothing? I've never heard you talk like this before."

"I don't know. Let's just get out of here. I think I might need your body, is all." My head was spinning. Being around all those rich people was making me feel some type of way. The only black faces in the house were mines and hers. That hurt me for some reason. I didn't know why, but it did.

* * *

As soon as we made it back to the stretch Navigator limousine, I knelt in front of Rayven, and held the box from Jacob's in her face. "Man, ma, I know this ain't the best proposal in the whole world, but I just want you to know that I love you, and that I'm riding wit you until the end. You've been my right-hand ever since we were kids, and I wanna make it official. I ain't trying to have you be just some baby mama. I want you to be my wife, and the mother of my child. Will you marry me?" I popped open the box and allowed the three-carat, pink lemonade, diamond ring, to dazzle in the light. She covered her mouth with her left hand, and slowly nodded her head.

"Yeah, boo. Yeah. I'll marry you. I'll be your wife." She knelt in front of me and kissed all over my lips. Wrapped her arms around my neck. I slid the ring on to her sized-seven finger and made sure that it was on there good. Picked her up and made her lean back. Took her tight Fendi skirt and lifted it all the way up to her hips. Then, I grabbed ahold of the crotch and pulled it upward so that the thongs were all in her ass, and a bit of the string separated her pussy lips.

They were meaty, and golden. Bald, and pretty. I placed my nose right on the front of her panties and sniffed hard, allowing her glorious aroma to waft up my nose, intoxicating me. "Daddy, you finna do that right here? You know our limo driver watching you right now?" In response, I moved the crotch band to the side, and licked up and down her slit. Tasting her salt, I sucked first the right lip into my mouth, and then the left one, pulling on them. Then I attacked her clit. Flickered it from side to side. It looked like a wet piece of meat. The little nib stood at attention. My tongue twirled around it, then I sucked it into my mouth. "Un! Daddy! He watching us. Fuck. He looking." She opened her legs wider, humped into my mouth, and moaned deep within her throat. "Daddy, do you hear me?" I spread her lips with my thumbs, exposing her pink. Her little hole came into view.

My tongue slid into it and traced the outer region. She jerked. Then, I was tongue fucking that pregnant pussy, making it ooze all over my chin. My nose smeared the juices over her waist line. I didn't care about the driver watching. It only added to the passion for me. "Un. Daddy. Daddy. Daddy. Aw fuck. I don't want him looking. Aw." She pulled down the straps to her skirt-dress. Her plump breasts popped out. The nipples erect. She pulled on the and opened her mouth wide. Breathing harder and harder. My tongue started to go crazy on her jewel below. "I'm finna cum. I'm finna cum. Daddy! I'm finna cum!" She wrapped her legs around my head and humped into my mouth hard. Cumming all over it. Nearly suffocating me. Her juices poured down my neck. Now I was hard and needed to be in her. Needed to be inside of her pregnant pussy. Because of her state, it made everything new to me. She was growing my child inside of her. There was nothing more special than that.

I picked her up and placed her on her knees in front of the mini bar. Got behind her and took my dick out. Slid it up and down her wet slit, while her titties bounced on her small frame. Slid in and grabbed her hips, sliding in and out of her at full speed. My dick forcing its way into her tight space. "Un. Daddy. Daddy. Oh fuck. Kaleb! Kaleb! Aw! I'm finna be! I'm finna be your wife, daddy!" She slammed back into me. This really made her titties bounce. After ten seconds of this, her scent got heavy in the limo. I knew the driver could smell it. I could only imagine what it did to him. One glance told me that he was peeping everything from his rear-view mirror.

I grabbed her hips and really got to going in. Feeling her pussy suck at me. It felt so good, my eyes rolled back in my head. I sped up the pace even more. Her big booty jiggled with each collision. I was close to skeeting all inside of her. I needed to. She looked back at me and sucked her bottom lip. Smashing backward. "Cum in me, daddy. Cum in me while he watch you fuck me like this. Aw shit!" She lowered her face to the floor and screamed. I slapped that big ass again and slid my thumb into her back door. The next thing I knew, I was cumming hard, while my body shook like crazy.

Chapter 14

"Yo, the way this shit go, we gotta make an example out of niggas. I hate when muhfuckas think it's sweet, because we getting money, so we gon' set the standard right now and carve these niggas like turkeys," Buddy said, snatching the black pillowcases off the men that he had tied up in the basement. I stepped behind him with a mug on my face.

"These the bitch niggas that been airing out our brownstones like it's sweet?" I asked, looking from one ugly face onto the next. All four had duct tape on their mouths, with sweat dripping down the sides of their faces. Buddy nodded.

"Hell, yeah. Blood 'nem gave me the footage of their whip speeding away on more than one occasion." He knelt down and took a knife out of a little tool box he had along the wall of the basement. The blade looked nine inches long, rugged, and sharp. He walked up to the first dark-skinned face and sliced the blade across his mug, then ripped the tape away from his mouth.

"Arrgh! Muthafucka!" he hollered. Blood gushed out of his wounds. "I was only doing what I was told. I don't even know you niggas," he spat, as the blood gushed into his eye, before he closed it. I stepped up to him and grabbed him by the neck, squeezed, and took the knife from Buddy.

"Who told you to clap at us, son? Huh? Spit that shit out." I placed the tip of the knife to his forehead and applied pressure. A slight trickle of blood appeared at the tip.

"Ah! Man, I ain't no snitch! I ain't no bitch nigga either. I ain't got shit to say." His chest heaved up and down.

"Oh, you don't?" I smacked him as hard as I could, then backhanded him to the floor. Buddy picked him up and sat him back in the chair. Then, I was standing in front of him again, ready to fuck him over. "Nigga, you wanna try this again?"

He coughed up blood and tried to breathe. "Look, man. If I talk, then I die. That's how the game go. It ain't shit you about to do to me that my chief won't." I slammed the knife in his thigh and ripped downward, slicing him all the way open. His jeans tore along with his skin. Blood skeeted upward and spilled over his leg. Dripped to the concrete and formed a puddle. He screamed at the top of his lungs, until Buddy punched him in the mouth with his wrist.

"Shut yo bitch ass up, making all that damn noise!" Buddy yelled.

"Aye, man, fuck this. Fuck this shit. It's Gorilla, kid. Son told us to sweat y'all shops. Told us to spray them bitches until they were shut down. I don't want this heat, Blood. I'm only sixteen." Buddy yanked the knife out of my hand.

"Nigga, fuck ya age." He took the knife and slammed it into the kid's throat, then kicked him in the center of his chest, knocking him backward. He wound up on the floor with blood skeeting out of his wounds like a geyser. I stood back with my eyes wide in disbelief. I didn't know if I was ready to ice these lil niggas, but apparently, Buddy was. He stood with the knife dripping blood, watching the lil nigga die. It was a sight to see.

I stepped to the next teen and ripped the tape from his mouth. Before I could say anything, he started to run his mouth a mile a minute. "Man, he gave us five hundred apiece. Told us to hit anybody we see. Made us threaten the hypes and all that shit. I don't want it wit you niggas, B. Yo, I saw y'all around Harlem all the time. If I wanted to sweat something, I would have back then, but that ain't me. I was bussing toward the ceilings of the traps, kid. That's my word," the yellow-faced lil nigga said with glossy eyes. He had two tear drops on the left side of his face. I knelt down eye level to him.

"Aw, so you was bussing to make sure you ain't hit nobody, huh? I guess you think that makes you less of my enemy, huh?" I curled my lip at him, disgusted by how quickly he was folding. He made Harlem look bad. I smelled snitch all over him. He shook his head. "I don't even know you to be your enemy, god. It's crazy out here. I couldn't pass up no five hundred. I was able to help my moms wit the rent because of that lil scratch. Word up." I shook my head.

"Yo, you made ya bed, son. You gotta lay in this bitch now. I can't feel sorry fa pussies like you. I just can't, kid." I took the knife from Buddy and held it tight in my hand.

"Come on, son, don't kill me, man. I got a bitch pregnant and all that shit. Don't take my life. Please. I'll do anything, boss. Just give me a chance," he whimpered. That crying shit had me vexed. Wasn't no man supposed to be acting how kid was. If I didn't have my mind set on stanking him before, now I did. One swipe with the wrist and the blade opened his throat wide. Blood poured out of the gash like some thick ass Kool-Aid, spilled down his chest, and into his lap. He blinked twice. Looked down at the blood, then up to me with tears in his eyes. He tried to say something, only more of his blood came from his lips. Then, his eyes closed, and he was out like a light. Buddy picked him up and threw his body on top of the first nigga he'd killed.

"Yo, I think that lil bitch nigga right there is Gorilla's nephew. Take his tape off, son, let's get the math on Blood," he said, pointing to the second to last shooter.

I rushed over to him and pulled off his tape. He was dark-skinned, heavyset, with a bald head, and a mouth full of gold. I found that out when he spoke his first words. "Yo, I don't give a fuck how much pain you fuck boys put me through. I ain't saying shit. It's Blood in, Blood out. Kill me and get this shit over with. Fuck both of you niggas. Suwoo!" He sucked his teeth and looked toward the ceiling with his head tilted backward. I laughed and looked over at Buddy.

"Kid, do you hear this lil nigga?" I asked, with a big smile on my face. Buddy stood by my side with a mug across his grill.

"Yeah, I heard what he said. This is definitely Gorilla's nephew. He look just like his punk ass. Let me see that knife, Dunn." I wiped the blood from the blade on Gorilla's nephew's face, then gave it to Buddy.

"Before you handle Blood, let me rap a taste wit him. Aight?"

"Yeah, but hurry up, son. I gotta murder on my mind. I hate that nigga Sheek's whole bloodline. Him and Gorilla." He looked at his wrist and balled his face into a snarl. I knelt in front of him.

"Yo, what Gorilla got against us?"

He looked off and turned his nose up. "Y'all gon' find out soon enough. Everybody know you niggas hit Sheek and the fam. That's how you niggas came up so quick. But yeah, karma is a bitch, nigga. A big black bitch nigga too. Word up." Buddy tried to move me out of the way.

"Yo, let me slice this tough ass nigga, Kaleb. He used enough of his word count." He swung the blade and because I pushed him backward, he was only able to swipe a piece of his cheek.

"Yo, go kill that fuck nigga right there. Let me chop it up wit this one. Just hold fast. Damn." Buddy spit on the floor.

"Fuck that, son." He rushed to the other victim, slammed the knife in his face, pulled it out, then slammed it back in again. The chair fell backwards. He straddled him and started to stab him over and over again. He was hitting him so much that his blood was popping into the air. Splattering against the walls. When he finished, he stood up and wiped his face with his wrist. "Hurry up with that nigga, kid. Straight up." Gorilla's nephew flared his nostrils, and blinked tears. "It is what it is."

"Yo, who saying we hit Sheek? Where that drag coming from?" I asked.

"Yo, Sheek's hit is the least of your worries, Blood. When them dread heads get ahold of your ass, it's gon' be one. The streets say you and this handless clown killed a boatload of their women. Left the kilos of heroin inside of them, just took their lives on some heinous shit. Man that's deep. They got killas coming from the island to crease both of you niggas and the bitches in ya families too. Once them dread heads get involved, it's curtains, kid. Case closed." I was taken aback. This was the first time I was hearing that we were being blamed for all of those Jamaican females Sheek had killed. And, I definitely didn't know that they'd had heroin in their bodies. Then why did Sheek gun them down. I was confused. Something wasn't adding up.

"Yo, we ain't kill them bitches, Sheek did. That's why my mans had to ice him. The streets got that shit wrong. That's on my daughter," Buddy said, dropping the knife in disbelief.

Gorilla's nephew looked off. "Nigga I ain't the one you gotta convince. It's a whole nation of killers that's screaming for you niggas' murders. Them, plus the Bloods out in Harlem. Y'all can kill me today, I'll see you on the other side real soon. Once you get there, I'ma buss ya ass. Word." I stood there perplexed. I didn't know what to do or say. Not only was we up against the Harlem Bloods, but now we were faced with a war against the dread heads. Shit was about to get real sticky, real fast. I had to think my way out of this shit.

"What we gon' do, man? We can't stay down here in this basement forever. Them niggas gon' start to stink in a minute. Let me off this peasant." I shook my head, and exhaled. "Look, son, I'ma do you a favor, if you do me one. Deal?"

"It depends on what you're talking about. Like I said, I'm ready to go right now. Fuck this life. Ain't nothing but pain here."

"Then let me kill him. Yo, I know you ain't about to save this nigga. Fuck that!" Buddy picked up the knife again.

"You send word back to Gorilla, let him know that we ain't have shit to do with those Jamaican women being killed. That his mans was responsible for that, that's why I took him out. Tell him that shit, and I'll let you walk out of here wit yo life, kid. That's my word."

"What? You gotta be fucking kidding me. Nigga, it's three bodies back there. Three. And you finna let this lil nigga walk away with his life. Really?"

"Yo, kid, shut the fuck up, nigga! Damn! Shut the fuck up and stand over there. I'm the head! Straight up!" I pointed. Buddy shook his head and followed my directives.

"Yo, this is dumb! The dumbest shit you ever did. That lil nigga walk out of here, he gon' tell everything. We gon' be on the run from the law, and all them niggas. Fuck!"

"Nigga, deal or no deal? I need to know right the fuck now," I said, facing the teen.

"Fuck what ya mans talking about, Kaleb. I ain't no snitch. You got a deal. I'll make sure Blood get the message. That's on my mother's grave." He spit blood on the floor and looked up at me.

"Aight then, it's a deal. Yo, Buddy, cut that nigga hand off and send him on his way. We ain't trying to have him be one of Gorilla's shooters somewhere down the line. Nah' mean?" The teen bucked his eyes, then nodded his head. "Yo, at least I'll have my life. Let's do it."

* * *

That night, I couldn't sleep. I tossed and turned in the bed. Sweating profusely. I kept having dreams that a bunch of dread headed niggas were chasing me with big sticks that had fire on the ends of them. I was running and looking for a weapon, but the streets were empty. Void of anything I could use to defend myself. At about three in the morning, Rayven jumped out of the bed and rushed into the bathroom. Pulled the toilet seat up and purged her guts. I rushed to her side to console her. Pulled her hair back, and held it for her until she finished. As soon as she did, I wiped her mouth with a warm rag, and kissed her soft cheek. She fell against my chest, breathing heavy. "Baby, it's good. I'm right here. I got you, goddess. You hear me?" I rubbed her arm and kissed her again.

"Yeah, daddy, I hear you, and I believe you too. I love you so much." She looked up at me and kissed my lips. Thought about the fact that she'd just puked and snapped her head back. "I'm sorry, baby. I forgot. I wasn't thinking, I swear."

"What?" I grabbed her to me, and slid my tongue into her mouth. Sucked all over her lips. Yeah, they tasted a little funny from her morning sickness, but I didn't care. I needed to let her know I had her. That I loved her and I'd be there to hold her down like a man was supposed to. She melted in my arms, and hugged, relieved. I could feel it in her body.

"Daddy, Sven bussed a move and acquired us a nice piece of property out in Queens. A house with four bedrooms, and two baths. A nice backyard, attic, and basement. I say we take it and hit her with half the money she's asking for it. Let's get our family nest together."

"How much scratch she talking?" I asked, helping her up.

"She wants five hundred thousand for anybody else, but I can get it for two hundred and fifty thousand, and trade her some other property for it. Rabbit still needs to lay low, so she'll be with us for about six months. You know, to help me get ready for the baby and all of that, but then, we'll be free to be alone. What do you think?" she asked, walking into the bedroom and sliding into the bed.

"Yo, as long as it'll make you happy, I'm good. I'll do whatever you need." I slid in the bed beside her.

"Good, because I already closed that deal. Plus, I got the girls working on something major that's about to turn New York upside down. I don't want to expose my hand just yet, but let's just say you're going to be proud of me. I promise."

Chapter 15

"Kaleb, I'm so glad that you're here. I been needing to see you so bad, come in," Bree said, pulling my wrist so I could step inside her new place that I'd help Buddy cop for her. Her hair looked freshly done. So did her nails. She smelled good, and looked even better. But there was a worried look on her face. She closed the door behind me, then looked out of the peep hole as if she were looking for somebody. That got me nervous. I slid my hand under my shirt, and gripped the handle of my nine millimeter. She turned back around, and exhaled. "Them Blood niggas been over here looking for you and my baby daddy. They didn't know what apartment I stayed in, so they knocked on damn near every door in the building until somebody led them to mine. I didn't even know the two that I saw through the peep hole, but their message was clear, when they saw the two of you, you were toast. The shorter, fat one threatened to kick my door in. I yelled that I was calling the police, and that's when they ran out of here. I don't know what y'all got going on, Kaleb, but I'm terrified."

She rushed into my arms and wrapped hers around me, holding me tight. The scent of her perfume went up my nose. She smelled so damn good. I took my hand off my pistol, and held her. Loving the feel of her softness. Hating the way she trembled. I didn't like them bitch niggas making the women in our circle worried about their lives. It made me feel like I was slipping. Like they felt them niggas were more monsters than me and Buddy was, and I didn't believe that for one second. I could get real bloody and vicious when I needed to be. She nuzzled her face into the crook of my neck and kissed me there. Her lips sucked, then her tongue licked up and down. My hands slid down and cuffed her ass.

It felt like it had gotten bigger over the past few months. She took a step back, and stood on her tippy toes, trying to kiss my lips. But, I moved my head out of the way, and released her. Turned my back on her, and sat on the couch. Left her standing there looking crazy. "Dang, I can't even get a kiss any more. You know I ain't been fucking Buddy, right?" She sat on the sofa next to me, and grabbed my left hand.

"I'm engaged to Rayven. I'm about to make her lil pretty ass my wife. She been stomp down. She deserve it." At least, that's how I feel. I could smell the scent of her. She was sitting too close. Had me feeling some type of way. For some reason, I had a crazy thing for Bree, and I was trying not to. Her caramel skin was just the right complexion, kind of dark. Her body was something to see, and the fact that she was born and raised in the projects gave us a connection. Then, there was the whole forbidden factor of things. She was Buddy's baby mother and I knew the homie was crazy like me. I knew the extent he would go through over her, and I guess a part of me got a thrill from the dangerous position I was placing myself in. Bree stood up, and frowned. Looked down on me with anger in her eyes.

"Are you serious? You're marrying her? Why? Is it because she's a red bone like all of you dudes be hollering is something so amazing?" She made air quotes with her fingers.

"Nall, it ain't got nothin' to do with that. Rayven just been one hunnit all around the board. She helping me excel in this game too. I can always depend on her. That's rare in a woman."

"Fuck that, Kaleb! You know the only reason me and you ain't together is because of Buddy! I been in love with your ass. Have been ever since I was a little girl, but you snubbed me for that half-breed bitch. That ain't fair. Dang, so where does that leave us? You ain't fucking wit me no more or something?" She ran her fingers through her hair in distress. I stood up.

"I don't know, but I ain't trying to do her wrong. I mean, we ain't even sat down and discussed what the monogamy side of things were going to look like. I don't know how she wanna play things. All I know is that I love her and I wanna make her happy. Plus, she pregnant with my seed." This was like a dagger to Bree's heart. She sat on the couch, and covered her mouth.

"I think I'm about to be sick, Kaleb." She lowered her head and covered her face with her hands. I sat next to her on the couch and rubbed her back.

I didn't want to hurt her, but I had to keep shit real wit her. I felt that she deserved the truth. Besides, sooner or later we had to stop going behind, Buddy's back anyway. "Yo, that don't mean I ain't gon' hold you down, Bree. I swear, for as long as I'm up, you will be too. I don't care what Buddy do for you, I'ma make sure you're good. You and Breeyonna. That's my word." She popped her head up.

"You think that all I care about is materialistic shit. Huh? You think I'm that fucking petty, Kaleb. Do you?" She rushed my hand away and stood back up. Pacing back and forth. "I don't want to be in the hood my whole life. I don't want to be a dependent. I want to be my own boss. To accomplish my own dreams. Real women don't need to depend on a man to support them. I'm not some fucking government assistance case. Damn." Her eyes got watery. "That mean I'm stuck with this bum-ass nigga? This addict? Really? Ugh, I hate life."

I got up. "Bree, you're overthinking things, ma. I'm fucking wit you on any level that you need me to be. Whatever your goals are, let me help you to reach them. I'll go out here and get this money, then I'll back you. I got you. Don't play me off like that. Come here." I held open my arms. She looked at me over her shoulders, and shook her head. Walked into my arms and hugged me.

"I ain't about to let you go like that, Kaleb. I know you love Rayven and all of that, but I love you, and I know you got mad love for me. You gotta have me too. I gotta be your woman too. She can have the ring. I just need to know that I'm in your heart. Please tell me that I am." She hugged me tighter, her voice started to break up. I took a deep breath, and shook my head within our embrace. Damn, it was so hard to be one hunnit to Rayven while I had Bree in my arms. And I know it wasn't right, but her vulnerability was getting the better of me. She was making me want her in the worst way.

"I know you got me, but I'd rather you help me to get myself. You can bring me a fish every day so I can eat and feed my daughter, or you can teach me how to fish so I can feed myself and my daughter. And if ever you should fall, then I could feed you back to strength as well." She kissed my lips slow and with so much passion, that I found myself breathing hard and gripping that big-ass booty. She slid her hands under my shirt and rubbed my chest, then pulled my shirt over my head. I placed my pistol on the table. Picked her up and laid her back on the couch. Got between her legs, pulled her wife beater up and sucked all over her pretty titties hungrily. The nipples covered most of the mounds. They looked like baby pacifiers, erect and rubbery. I pulled on them with my lips, and trailed my tongue around them over and over. She arched her back.

"That's what I'm talking about, Kaleb. Your touch. Your touch is so amazing. I've never felt anything like you before," she moaned. Slid her hand between her legs, into her tight shorts rubbing herself.

"Let me taste 'em, baby. Let me taste them fingers," I crooned, opening my mouth for her to park them inside for me. She ran her fingers under my nose, and then into my mouth. I sucked her juices off of them. Could smell her secret scent. It made my piece harder and harder. Finally, I couldn't take it no more. I yanked her shorts off of her, and pulled them off her ankles. Opened her thick thighs wide, and stuck my face between them, sucking all over her dark brown pussy that was lightly trimmed. Sucked on the lips and watched them pop back into place after they exited my lips with a sucking pop.

"Un! Kaleb! I love you so much! She can have the ring. She can have it. I just want you. I just want my portion of you. Please!"

My face went from side to side. My tongue out, and licking, hitting her clit on target, causing her to squirm all over the place, as bad as she was wanting me. I kept seeing Rayven's face in my mind. The pink lemonade diamond ring, and the vision of her throwing up on the floor from morning sickness. The effects of preparing our child a home within her stomach. Damn, it was all so mentally draining. I loved Rayven so much.

"Well, am I, Kaleb? Am I in your heart? Do you really love me? I need to hear you say it. Don't look down on me because I ain't got nothing right now. My time is coming. I just need to get out of this impossible situation with Buddy. That's all." I kissed her neck, and took a whiff of her as I inhaled deeply.

"Yeah, I love you, Bree. I love you, and you have a major piece of my heart. I see your struggles, ma. I know you're down right now, but not for long. I ain't about to turn my back on you. I promise." I held her tighter. "Anything you need, ma, it's yours, word is bond." I didn't know what to do. I was so confused and double-minded. Being there with her, I started to imagine how I could make her life better. How I could help her rise to the top of the game in her own lane. I knew how it felt to be from the projects when everything seemed out of reach, when you felt that all you could ever be was trash. I liked the fact that she wanted more. That she didn't want to settle for less. That she didn't want to be a dependent. That she wanted to get up and do her own thing. That was hot to me. That attracted me to her. It attracted me to her more than I wanted to admit. She slid out of my arms, and looked up at me with her pretty brown eyes, and the light freckles all over her face that you could only see when you were as close as we were.

"Kaleb, I know it ain't right, but I love you. You're not like all of these other low-life dudes that are all around New York. You're a man. You've been helping me to take care of Breeyonna ever since she's been born. You've been more of a help to me than her own father. I wish we would have never broken up back in the day."

Her thick thighs gyrated into my face. Humping me, until she came screaming, forcing me further inside of her wet box. "Kaleb! Kaleb! Kaleb!" she hollered. I stood up, and undid my things, pulled my piece out and stroked him up and down. She reached and took ahold of it. Pumping it in her little fist. Tugged on it and made me sit back on the couch. She crawled between my legs and sucked the head into her mouth, and started to spear her head in my lap, making loud, gross, sucking noises.

My toes were curled. I gripped the sofa cushions, and all I could think about was my own pleasure. I wanted to cum in her mouth. I had to. I wanted see her jaws fill up with my semen and spill over. She was so fine. I knew that sight would do somethin' to me. She nipped the head with her teeth, then twisted the skin on my piece and deep throated me over and over. The sounds of her gagging pushed me over the edge. I couldn't take it no more. I had to cum. "Yo, I'm cumming, Bree. I'm coming, ma. Fuck!" I groaned, and started humping my hips off of the couch. She took the first squirts with her lips pursed together on top of my helmet. Then she removed her mouth, and jagged my pipe, while cum flew into her mouth from about a foot back. Some landed on her cheek, but she kept on jagging, before sucking me back into her mouth again, and going to town. This made my shit harder than ever. I wanted to fuck her hard. "Get yo ass up here and ride me! Now! Get yo ass up here!"

She straddled my lap, and held my dick while she slid down on me. Her pussy felt like an oven turned on broil. The walls were silky. Full of cushion, and it felt tight in her box. Like a fist. She sat all the way up and started to twerk while she rode me. Her big booty jiggled. She held the back of the couch for support and went crazy. "Un. Un. Aw! Aw! Kaleb! Kaleb! I love you. I love you so much. This pussy yours. Fuck Buddy! This pussy yours!" She twerked harder and harder. I could feel the couch moving backward into the wall. Once there, it started to knock against it. My dick ran in and out of her at full speed. Her juices ran into my lap and spilled on to the couch pillows. I humped upward to meet her downward thrusts, trying to hit her rock bottom with success.

"Bree. Bree. I'm about to cum in this pussy, ma. I'm about to cum. Get up." I felt my cum rising in my balls. It was coming all the way from the pits of my stomach. My vision was getting blurry. That project pussy had me going through one. "Arrgh!" She wrapped her arms around my neck and started to twerk so hard that her ass was slapping her back before she popped it forward, riding me like a jockey. She licked my cheek, then bit into my neck.

"Cum in me! Cum in me, Kaleb! Shit!" Faster and faster she went, forcing my seed out of my penis. I tried to get up to throw her off of me, but she had me pinned. My body shook and the next thing I knew, I was cumming in spasms.

"Uh. Uh. Uh. Bree. Fuck. Bitch, you made me. Shit," I said through clenched teeth. I could feel her walls milking, sucking the life out of my pole, while she humped harder and harder.

"Kaleb! Baby! I'm cumming! I'm cumming! Aw fuck, nigga! Shit!" Her pussy got so wet that I could hear the smacking sounds of it. It sounded like bare feet running on the side of a swimming pool. She licked my neck, and came harder and harder. Screaming. Then fell against me, out of breath. Her breath smelled like cinnamon.

* * *

We sat there connected for another ten minutes, not saying a word, but both knowing that we'd somehow crossed another line. Finally, I patted her ass. "Get up, ma. I gotta get out of here." She slowly climbed off of me. My dick slipped out of her hole, and slapped against my thigh. I looked between her legs at her gap as she sat on the couch and saw that her lips were slightly opened enough for me to see her bubble gum pink. The brown lips slowly covered the window to her insides. It looked hot to me. The female sex was wonderfully made.

"Kaleb, so where do we go from here? I mean, I just gotta know?" she asked, standing up with her hand between her legs. Rubbing her kitty that I was sure hurt just a bit. I headed toward the bathroom so I could wash up. I had to stay fresh at all times. I didn't like the thought of walking around with the scent of sex on me.

"Yo, it's just like I said, Bree. I care about you. And I'ma hold you down. I don't know what I'ma do about Buddy just yet, or Rayven, but as far as we go, I got you. Put your game plan together to perfect your goals and I'ma help you achieve them. We are bigger than the projects. You hear me?" She nodded from the couch and smiled.

"I love you so much. I won't fail you. I promise." Made her way over and kissed my lips. Hugged me, and exhaled loudly.

"It ain't about failing me, it's about failing you. You gotta be first, ma, then Breeyonna. You will only soar as high as you believe you can." I hugged her, and went into the bathroom and washed up. I was just placing my pistol on my hip when there was a banging on the front door.

T.J. Edwards

Chapter 16

Bree ran out of the bedroom with a pair of jogging pants on and a white beater. Her braless breasts were bouncing in her shirt. Both nipples present under the fabric. "Oh my God. Who is that? Who is that, Kaleb?" Before I could answer that question, the pounding commenced again. This time it was louder and harder. I led the way with my gun, and pushed Bree into her bedroom. "Don't come out of that room until I tell you to. Get down, and close this door. She rushed and kissed my lips, then ran into the room and slammed the door. I crept closer and closer to the front door. Got about two feet away when the banging ensued again.

"Yo, who the fuck is it?" I hollered, cocking the hammer on my gun and pointing my piece at the door.

"Yo, open the fucking door. It's Buddy, nigga. Fuck!" came Buddy's voice on the other side. I looked around the living room for any signs that me and Bree had been fucking. Finding none, I placed my eye on the peep hole and almost lost my breath. There in the hallway stood Buddy. Beside him, was Gorilla. He had a double barrel shotgun pressed under Buddy's chin. There were two other men in the hall as well. Both had red rags covering their faces. "Open the fucking door, Kaleb. Damn, nigga!" His head was tilted to the side to accommodate the long barrel of Gorilla's weapon.

"Yo, what's good? Why the fuck y'all got my mans hemmed up like that?" I asked, feeling my heart beat rapid in my chest. I was about to panic. I didn't know what to do. I rushed over to the window and looked out, saw Gorilla's black Ford Aerostar van that he used to kidnap Crips and other enemies of his mob.

"Yo, hand to God, if you don't open this door, I'ma blow ya man's shit out all over this hallway, then we gone sweat

159

you too. Right now, all I wanna do is talk. But, you're making me angry." Fuck. Sweat came down the side of my face. I had been plugged under Gorilla long enough to know that that fool ain't just want to talk. He had way more on his mind than that, I was sure of it. I didn't know if I was supposed to open the door and risk them killing Buddy and then me, or not open the door and risk them killing Buddy, and still sweating the house. I had Bree in the back room. She was the mother of my goddaughter, and a female I cared about.

I had to keep her wellbeing, and my own at the forefront of my mind. I couldn't be stupid. "Kaleb, this how you gon' leave ya home boy out here, son? Some kind of friend you are. Yo, if he don't open this door in the next thirty seconds, I'm blowing ya wig off, Buddy. That's my word. You hear that, Kaleb?" Bree came out of the back room.

"Kaleb, who is that at the door?" she cried, with her finger in her mouth. I waved her off and pointed for her to go back into the room.

"Aight, Gorilla. Aight. Yo, I'm about to open the door, just take that gun away from my nigga's head. That's all I ask."

"You got twenty seconds, Kaleb. Open this muthafuckin' door, or this nigga is a goner! Word!" he hollered. I placed my hand on the lock, closed my eyes and took a deep breath. Fuck, here goes nothing. Before I turned the lock, I heard the sound of cars rolling up to the front of Bree's house and slamming on their brakes.

I rushed to the window and saw three car loads of dread heads step out of their whips with assault rifles in their hands. Then, they were running up toward Bree's brownstone with Jamaican flags wrapped around the lower portion of their faces like masks. My heart dropped into my stomach. It was time to go to war, and let the shells drop where they may.

To Be Continued...
Rise to Power 2
Coming Soon

Submission Guideline

Submit the first three chapters of your completed manuscript to ldpsubmissions@gmail.com, subject line: Your book's title. The manuscript must be in a .doc file and sent as an attachment. Document should be in Times New Roman, double spaced and in size 12 font. Also, provide your synopsis and full contact information. If sending multiple submissions, they must each be in a separate email.

Have a story but no way to send it electronically? You can still submit to LDP/Ca$h Presents. Send in the first three chapters, written or typed, of your completed manuscript to:

LDP: Submissions Dept
Po Box 870494
Mesquite, Tx 75187

DO NOT send original manuscript. Must be a duplicate.

Provide your synopsis and a cover letter containing your full contact information.

Thanks for considering LDP and Ca$h Presents.

<u>Coming Soon from Lock Down Publications/Ca$h Presents</u>

BOW DOWN TO MY GANGSTA

By **Ca$h**

TORN BETWEEN TWO

By **Coffee**

BLOOD STAINS OF A SHOTTA **III**

By **Jamaica**

STEADY MOBBIN **III**

By **Marcellus Allen**

BLOOD OF A BOSS **V**

By **Askari**

LOYAL TO THE GAME **IV**

LIFE OF SIN II

By **T.J. & Jelissa**

A DOPEBOY'S PRAYER **II**

By **Eddie "Wolf" Lee**

IF LOVING YOU IS WRONG... **III**

LOVE ME EVEN WHEN IT HURTS **II**

By **Jelissa**

TRUE SAVAGE **VI**

By **Chris Green**

BLAST FOR ME **III**

A BRONX TALE III

DUFFLE BAG CARTEL

By **Ghost**

ADDICTIED TO THE DRAMA **III**

T.J. Edwards

By **Jamila Mathis**
LIPSTICK KILLAH **III**
WHAT BAD BITCHES DO **III**
KILL ZONE **II**
By **Aryanna**
THE COST OF LOYALTY **II**
By **Kweli**
SHE FELL IN LOVE WITH A REAL ONE **II**
By **Tamara Butler**
LOVE SHOULDN'T HURT **III**
RENEGADE BOYS **III**
By **Meesha**
CORRUPTED BY A GANGSTA **IV**
By **Destiny Skai**
A GANGSTER'S CODE **III**
By **J-Blunt**
KING OF NEW YORK IV
RISE TO POWER II
By **T.J. Edwards**
GORILLAS IN THE BAY II
De'Kari
THE STREETS ARE CALLING II
Duquie Wilson
KINGPIN KILLAZ III
Hood Rich
STEADY MOBBIN' **III**
Marcellus Allen

164

Rise to Power

SINS OF A HUSTLA II
ASAD
CASH MONEY HOES
Nicole Goosby
TRIGGADALE II
Elijah R. Freeman

Available Now
RESTRAINING ORDER **I & II**
By **CA$H & Coffee**
LOVE KNOWS NO BOUNDARIES **I II & III**
By **Coffee**
RAISED AS A GOON I, II, III & IV
BRED BY THE SLUMS I, II, III
BLAST FOR ME I & II
ROTTEN TO THE CORE I III
A BRONX TALE I, II
By **Ghost**
LAY IT DOWN **I & II**
LAST OF A DYING BREED
BLOOD STAINS OF A SHOTTA I & II
By **Jamaica**
LOYAL TO THE GAME
LOYAL TO THE GAME II
LOYAL TO THE GAME III
LIFE OF SIN

T.J. Edwards

By **TJ & Jelissa**
BLOODY COMMAS I & II
SKI MASK CARTEL I II & III
KING OF NEW YORK I II,III
RISE TO POWER

By **T.J. Edwards**
IF LOVING HIM IS WRONG…I & II
LOVE ME EVEN WHEN IT HURTS
By **Jelissa**
WHEN THE STREETS CLAP BACK I & II III
By **Jibril Williams**
A DISTINGUISHED THUG STOLE MY HEART I II & III
LOVE SHOULDN'T HURT I II
RENEGADE BOYS I & II
By **Meesha**
A GANGSTER'S CODE I & II
By J-Blunt
PUSH IT TO THE LIMIT
By **Bre' Hayes**
BLOOD OF A BOSS **I, II, III & IV**
By **Askari**
THE STREETS BLEED MURDER **I, II & III**
THE HEART OF A GANGSTA I II& III
By **Jerry Jackson**
CUM FOR ME
CUM FOR ME 2

166

CUM FOR ME 3

CUM FOR ME 4

An **LDP Erotica Collaboration**

BRIDE OF A HUSTLA **I II & II**

THE FETTI GIRLS **I, II& III**

CORRUPTED BY A GANGSTA I, II & III

By **Destiny Skai**

WHEN A GOOD GIRL GOES BAD

By **Adrienne**

A GANGSTER'S REVENGE **I II III & IV**

THE BOSS MAN'S DAUGHTERS

THE BOSS MAN'S DAUGHTERS II

THE BOSSMAN'S DAUGHTERS III

THE BOSSMAN'S DAUGHTERS IV

THE BOSS MAN'S DAUGHTERS **V**

A SAVAGE LOVE **I & II**

BAE BELONGS TO ME

A HUSTLER'S DECEIT I, II

WHAT BAD BITCHES DO I, II

By **Aryanna**

A KINGPIN'S AMBITON

A KINGPIN'S AMBITION **II**

I MURDER FOR THE DOUGH

By **Ambitious**

TRUE SAVAGE

TRUE SAVAGE II

TRUE SAVAGE **III**

TRUE SAVAGE **IV**

TRUE SAVAGE **V**

By **Chris Green**

A DOPEBOY'S PRAYER

By **Eddie "Wolf" Lee**

THE KING CARTEL **I, II & III**

By **Frank Gresham**

THESE NIGGAS AIN'T LOYAL **I, II & III**

By **Nikki Tee**

GANGSTA SHYT **I II &III**

By **CATO**

THE ULTIMATE BETRAYAL

By **Phoenix**

BOSS'N UP **I , II & III**

By **Royal Nicole**

I LOVE YOU TO DEATH

By Destiny J

I RIDE FOR MY HITTA

I STILL RIDE FOR MY HITTA

By **Misty Holt**

LOVE & CHASIN' PAPER

By **Qay Crockett**

TO DIE IN VAIN

SINS OF A HUSTLA

By **ASAD**

BROOKLYN HUSTLAZ

By **Boogsy Morina**

Rise to Power

BROOKLYN ON LOCK I & II
By **Sonovia**
GANGSTA CITY
By **Teddy Duke**
A DRUG KING AND HIS DIAMOND I & II III
A DOPEMAN'S RICHES
HER MAN, MINE'S TOO I, II
By Nicole Goosby
TRAPHOUSE KING **I II & III**
KINGPIN KILLAZ
By **Hood Rich**
LIPSTICK KILLAH **I, II**
CRIME OF PASSION I & II
By **Mimi**
STEADY MOBBN' **I, II**
By **Marcellus Allen**
WHO SHOT YA **I, II**
Renta
GORILLAZ IN THE BAY
DE'KARI
TRIGGADALE
Elijah R. Freeman
GOD BLESS THE TRAPPERS I, II, III
THESE SCANDALOUS STREETS I, II, III
FEAR MY GANGSTA I, II, III
THESE STREETS DON'T LOVE NOBODY I, II
Tranay Adams

THE STREETS ARE CALLING

Duquie Wilson

BOOKS BY LDP'S CEO, CA$H

TRUST IN NO MAN
TRUST IN NO MAN 2
TRUST IN NO MAN 3
BONDED BY BLOOD
SHORTY GOT A THUG
THUGS CRY
THUGS CRY 2
THUGS CRY 3
TRUST NO BITCH
TRUST NO BITCH 2
TRUST NO BITCH 3
TIL MY CASKET DROPS
RESTRAINING ORDER
RESTRAINING ORDER 2
IN LOVE WITH A CONVICT

Coming Soon
BONDED BY BLOOD 2
BOW DOWN TO MY GANGSTA

T.J. Edwards